"So you won't marry me?"

"No."

"What about your financial problems?"

"I'm looking for a job, not a meal ticket," Lizzy said coldly. "I'm sorry if you feel you've wasted an expensive bottle of champagne on me, but you're going to have to look elsewhere for a wife. I'm not for sale."

Wearily, she made to push back her chair, but Tye caught her wrist.

"Lizzy, wait! You want a job? I'll give you a job. If you won't marry me yourself, you can find me someone who will."

OUTBACK
Brides

In the hot, dusty Australian Outback,
the last thing a woman expects to find is a husband....

Clare, the Englishwoman, Ellie, the tomboy
and Lizzy, the career girl, don't come to this harsh,
beautiful land looking for love.

Yet they all find themselves saying "I do"
to a handsome Australian man of their dreams!

In January
Baby at Bushman's Creek

In March
Wedding at Waverley Creek

In May
A Bride for Barra Creek

Welcome to an exciting new trilogy by rising star
Jessica Hart

Celebrate three unexpected weddings, Australian-style!

A BRIDE FOR BARRA CREEK

Jessica Hart

OUTBACK *Brides*

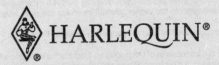

HARLEQUIN®

TORONTO • NEW YORK • LONDON
AMSTERDAM • PARIS • SYDNEY • HAMBURG
STOCKHOLM • ATHENS • TOKYO • MILAN • MADRID
PRAGUE • WARSAW • BUDAPEST • AUCKLAND

For Annie, with love on reaching Chapter Ten.

ISBN 0-373-03654-X

A BRIDE FOR BARRA CREEK

First North American Publication 2001.

Copyright © 2001 by Jessica Hart.

CHAPTER ONE

'YOU may kiss the bride.'

Smiling, Lizzy watched as Jack cupped Ellie's face between his hands and bent his head to kiss her. It was only a brief kiss, but Lizzy was sure that for that moment the two of them had completely forgotten their audience and existed only for each other.

Lucky Ellie, thought Lizzy as she saw Jack's hand close firmly around her sister's, and she couldn't help wondering a little wistfully if it would ever be her turn. When was she going to find someone who belonged with her the way Jack belonged with Ellie?

Not that she didn't have more important things to worry about, Lizzy reminded herself. Like finding a job. Falling in love would be wonderful, but it wouldn't pay off her credit card bills, would it?

Lizzy's mind flickered towards the likely total, and veered away like a startled horse. She shouldn't have bought those shoes, she thought, glancing down at them a little guiltily. They had been an extravagance, but they were perfect with the dress, and she'd had to look nice for Ellie's wedding. It wasn't every day your little sister got married.

Anyway, Lizzy decided firmly, she wasn't going to think about her overdraft today. This was Ellie's day.

Blue eyes warm with affection, Lizzy looked around the old woolshed. It looked as if the entire district had turned out to see Ellie marry Jack Henderson. How could their marriage fail to be a success when so many people were there to wish them well? All the faces were familiar to Lizzy, all were smiling.

Except one.

He was standing on his own, not talking, not smiling, just surveying the scene with an air of detached cynicism that made him stand out from the crowd far more than his height or his dark, harsh features.

As a child, Lizzy had been sent a book of fairy tales from England. It had been illustrated with green fields and dense, dark forests that had meant little to a child growing up in the outback. One of the pictures had shown a wolf, barely disguised beneath a fleece, prowling through a field of sheep. It had conveyed the same sense of lurking menace that Lizzy felt now, staring at the stranger, and a tiny shiver tiptoed down her spine.

The photographer was busily arranging family groups and Lizzy was called just then to stand next to her sister. Smiling obediently for the camera, she craned her neck slightly to keep the mysterious stranger in view over the photographer's shoulder, and her interest deepened when she saw the way the other guests eyed him askance and were careful to give him a wide berth. Clearly she wasn't the only one who sensed something different about him, something dangerous, yet strangely compelling.

Released by the photographer, Lizzy manoeuvred her way to the edge of the group where she could greet guests waiting to congratulate Jack and Ellie and watch the man at the same time. He had acquired a glass of the champagne that was circulating, and judging by the curl of his lip he didn't think much of it.

Lizzy was intrigued. Who was he? His hair was dark and cut close to his head, his face angular, with strong features and a forbidding expression. He might be dressed like all the other men in the room, but there was an unmistakably maverick quality about him. It was something to do with the hardness of his mouth, with the coiled power that was evident in the way he held himself, with the cool, watchful eyes.

Her mother must know who he was, Lizzy reasoned. He didn't look like the kind of man who would drive thirty miles from the nearest sealed road to gatecrash an ordinary outback wedding, so presumably he had been invited.

She turned to ask, but her mother was talking to the celebrant, and when she glanced back to the stranger she found herself looking straight into his eyes. They were piercingly pale in his dark face, and so cold that Lizzy's heart jerked and the breath dried in her throat.

She had the oddest feeling that the floor of the woolshed had dropped away beneath her feet and only that unnervingly light gaze was holding her above an abyss. It could only have been for a moment, but to Lizzy it felt as if she hung there for ever, her gaze locked with his.

And then he smiled, a swift, mocking smile that for some reason sent the colour surging into her cheeks. Lizzy wrenched her eyes away and pointedly turned her back, furious to find that her heart was hammering in her chest.

It hadn't been a nice smile. Not really. She wasn't even going to ask who he was. From now on, she decided, she would ignore him.

Only somehow she couldn't. Lizzy threw herself into her role as bridesmaid, flitting between groups, hugging old friends, laughing, kissing, agreeing that Ellie looked beautiful and that she and Jack were perfect for each other, but no matter how many times she tried to turn her back, the stranger always seemed to be there, lurking irritatingly at the edge of her vision.

Perversely, the moment she couldn't see him any more, she missed him. On her way back from the bar that had been set up at one end of the woolshed, Lizzy paused and sipped her champagne, surveying the crowd with a slight frown between her brows. Where had he gone?

'Looking for me?' a voice said in her ear, and Lizzy started, the champagne sloshing out of her glass as she swung round.

Sure enough, it was the stranger, looking even more sardonic at close quarters. Close to, Lizzy could see that his eyes were grey, but so light they seemed glacial against the darkness of his hair and lashes, and she had the uncomfortable feeling that they could see right through her.

'Why should I be looking for *you*?' she asked, with what she thought was creditable coolness considering that her heart seemed to have taken up residence in her throat, where it was jumping and fluttering and generally making it ridiculously hard for her to breathe.

'I'm the only person here you haven't kissed,' he said. He had an unusual accent, not wholly Australian nor completely American, but somewhere in between. 'You wouldn't want to miss anyone out, would you?'

Lizzy swallowed her heart firmly. 'I only kiss people I know,' she said, 'and I don't know you.'

'We could introduce ourselves,' he pointed out. 'Although I already know exactly who you are.'

Lizzy, opening her mouth to reply to his suggestion, was thrown. 'You do?' she asked uncertainly.

'I've been asking around about you. You're Elizabeth

Walker, always known as Lizzy, elder sister of the bride and all round nice girl.'

For some reason this description annoyed Lizzy. 'That's not quite how I'd describe myself,' she said with something of a snap.

'Oh? How would you describe yourself?'

'As a professional woman,' said Lizzy loftily and not very accurately. 'I'm in PR.'

'Ah.' He nodded down at her feet. 'That explains the shoes.'

In spite of herself, Lizzy warmed to him. He was the only person who had noticed her shoes. Following his gaze downwards, she couldn't help smiling. There was just something *about* shoes, Lizzy felt. You couldn't put on a pair like this and not feel good.

'Aren't they wonderful?' she said, forgetting for a moment that she didn't like him.

His eyes travelled slowly up from the shoes to her face. Lizzy was tall and built on generous lines. Whenever she grumbled about losing weight, her friends would roll their eyes and assure her that her figure was perfectly proportioned to her height and her personality. Deep down, Lizzy knew that this was true, but it didn't stop her grumbling. She was normal, after all.

For Ellie's wedding she had found a fabulous dress that emphasised her warm curves and glowing, opulent skin. Kingfisher-blue, its colour intensified the blueness of her eyes and made a wonderful foil for her wavy blonde hair, bluntly cut to her chin, and her stylishly bold lipstick.

There was no way that Lizzy could be described as a classical beauty, but her face was so vivid that no one ever noticed that her nose was too big and her mouth too wide or that there were already lines starring the edges of her eyes.

'Wonderful,' Tye agreed. His face was quite straight, but something in his voice set a blush stealing into Lizzy's cheeks, and she looked quickly away. It was a relief when his gaze dropped back to her shoes. 'But not very practical,' he added.

They certainly weren't. She had nearly twisted her ankle several times on the uneven woolshed floor. To her chagrin, Lizzy realised that she had been holding her breath and let it out. 'There are more important things in life than practicality,' she said firmly, and a disconcerting gleam of amusement lit the cool grey eyes.

'You must be the only person in this woolshed to think so!'

That was probably true too, Lizzy reflected, glancing around at the people she had grown up with. They were all wonderful, and she loved them deeply, but they didn't understand about shoes.

'You have to be practical if you live in the outback,' she said, her gaze coming back to meet his almost defiantly. 'I don't. I'm a city girl now.'

'So I gathered.'

Lizzy didn't quite know what to make of that. There had been an odd undercurrent to his voice that she couldn't interpret. 'You seem to know all about me,' she pointed out with a challenging look, 'but I still don't know who you are.'

'I'm Tye Gibson,' he told her, and he smiled sardonically at the expression on her face. 'Yes, *that* Tye Gibson,' he answered her unspoken question. 'Didn't anyone tell you that the black sheep of the district was back?'

'No,' admitted Lizzy, too surprised to think what she was saying.

She couldn't help staring. Tye Gibson! No one had seen him since he had walked off his family property nearly twenty years ago, but of course they all knew about him. Breaking off all contact with his father, Tye had turned his back on the bush and gone on make his fortune. Not just an ordinary little fortune, not just millions, but *serious* money.

Lizzy had never been absolutely sure what Tye Gibson did—something to do with communications, she thought—but she knew that his company, GCS, was a global giant, and that his name was a byword for ruthlessness around the world. It wasn't bad going for a boy from Barra Creek, but nobody wanted to claim him as a local hero. However Tye had made his fortune, it hadn't been by being nice.

It seemed that anyone who ever had to do business with him regretted it, and the press didn't like him any better. Refusing to be interviewed or photographed, Tye Gibson was apparently content for people to think of him as heartless and amoral, and the richer and more reclusive he became, the more the myths about him proliferated.

Nor did the district he had grown up in have anything good to say for him. Lizzy had been a little girl when he'd left his father to struggle on his own, and anyway had never met him, but gossip travelled fast around the outback and she knew all about his unsavoury reputation. Nobody had been sorry to see him go.

But now it seemed that he was back—and it wasn't hard to guess why.

'Aren't you a little late?' she said.

Tye's dark brows lifted. 'What do you mean?'

'Your father's funeral was a week ago,' said Lizzy pointedly.

'So?'

'So couldn't you have made the effort to get here in time for that?'

His face hardened. 'I think that would have been a little hypocritical, don't you? My father and I hadn't spoken for twenty years. What would have been the point of me weeping crocodile tears over the coffin? Besides,' he went on, glancing around him, 'I doubt if I would have been very welcome. That's been made very obvious today.'

'Are you surprised?'

'Not in the slightest.' There was a cynical twist to Tye's lips. 'Nothing's changed round here. I never expected to be greeted as the prodigal son.'

'Perhaps if you'd come back to see your father when he was alive, you would have been,' said Lizzy tartly.

She must have drunk more champagne than she'd thought. She wasn't usually like this. Normally she had the sunniest of natures and wanted everyone to like her, but there was something about Tye Gibson that got under her skin and left her feeling ruffled and somehow aggravated.

'He wanted to see you,' she told Tye, who lifted a disbelieving eyebrow.

'Did he?'

Lizzy lost some of her assurance. 'Well…that's what I heard. I heard that he'd begged you to come home so that he could see you before he died.'

Tye laughed, but there was no humour in it. 'I'd like to have seen my father begging for anything!'

It didn't ring that true with what Lizzy remembered

of Frank Gibson either, now that he mentioned it. Frank had been a proud man.

'You mean it's not true?'

'Asking me to post a letter would have been giving in as far as my father was concerned,' said Tye flatly.

Lizzy hesitated. 'If he was dying, he might have looked at things differently,' she suggested, but Tye only smiled ironically.

'You didn't know my father very well, did you?'

She looked at him in some puzzlement. 'What are you doing here, then?'

'I've come to sort out my father's affairs,' he said. 'And to see Barra again.'

'But I thought—'

Lizzy stopped, uncomfortably aware that she was repeating gossip.

'You thought what? That my father had disinherited me?'

'Well…yes,' she admitted awkwardly.

Frank had made no secret of the fact that he had been bitterly hurt by his son's rejection, and when Tye hadn't come back when he was dying everyone had naturally assumed that he would do as he had long threatened and cut Tye out of his will.

'No, he didn't do that,' said Tye, but his mouth was set in a grim line and Lizzy wondered what he was thinking about. It wasn't anything nice, that was for sure.

What kind of man would refuse to visit his dying father? That had been cruel. She eyed him speculatively from under her lashes. No one had been the least bit surprised at his non-appearance, but it seemed to Lizzy that his face didn't really live up to his reputation. It was guarded, yes, shuttered and stubborn, but it wasn't cruel. He had the dark, difficult look of a wild horse that had refused to be broken, she thought. His mouth was hard, but maybe it hadn't always been that way.

Maybe it would look quite different if he were happy. Lizzy's blue eyes rested on his mouth, trying to imagine him smiling—not a cynical, mocking smile, but a real smile. What would make him smile like that? A woman? Maybe love? Lizzy found herself imagining what it would be like to see his face soften and his mouth curve, and something stirred treacherously inside her.

Jerking her gaze away, she took a slug of champagne. This was Tye Gibson, remember? Rumour was that he had had his heart surgically removed a long time ago. His idea of happiness was probably a nice day spent asset-stripping a company, followed by a relaxing hour of currency speculation.

A spoon was being banged against a glass for attention, and her father was climbing onto a chair to make a speech. Lizzy's eyes softened as she watched him. Dear old Dad, so calm and quiet and unflappable. She would be lost without him. She couldn't *imagine* not speaking to him for twenty years.

Her father was followed by Jack, who was very funny and made everyone laugh. He finished by toasting Lizzy as bridesmaid and they all clapped and cheered, turning to lift their glasses to where she stood with Tye at the edge of the woolshed.

'To Lizzy!' they cried, but she was uneasily aware that Tye was not included in their smiles.

Laughing, she blew a kiss of acknowledgment to Jack, but she was glad when everyone turned back to the bride and groom once more.

She slid a glance from under her lashes at Tye. In his place she would have been mortified by the obvious way he had been ignored, but Tye's expression gave absolutely nothing away. Lizzy was sure that he had noticed, though. Those watchful eyes would miss nothing.

'Lizzy!' Ellie was calling her over the crowd, and Lizzy looked quickly away from Tye to see her sister waving her bouquet. 'Catch!' she shouted.

The flowers came sailing through the air towards her, ribbons fluttering. Instinctively, Lizzy thrust her glass into Tye's hand and jumped, catching the bouquet between both hands, and the room cheered as she flourished them triumphantly.

'Your turn next!' someone called, and she laughed.

'I wish!'

Her face was still alight with laughter as she turned back to Tye. He was watching her with an expression so peculiar that her smile slowly faded. 'Thanks,' she said, looking at the glass he still held, and he gave it back to her as if he had forgotten that he had it.

There was a pause. Lizzy was very conscious of Tye's eyes boring into her face, and she put her glass down so that she could fiddle with the flowers. For some reason she couldn't look at him.

'I suppose you think this kind of thing is all very silly,' she said, a defensive edge to her voice.

'Why do you say that?'

'You don't believe in marriage.'

'How do you know that?'

Lizzy thought of all the beautiful women who had been out with Tye and then appeared in the gossip columns, complaining about his coldness, his selfishness, his callous refusal to commit to a relationship. It had always been a wonder to Lizzy that they could all sound so aggrieved by their failure to turn a heartless recluse into a party-going romantic. It wasn't as if they couldn't have known exactly what to expect.

'I've read about you in the papers,' she admitted.

'Oh, the *papers*!' Tye didn't even bother to conceal his sarcasm. 'It must be true, then!'

'Isn't it?'

He shrugged. 'Let's say that I have trouble understanding what all the fuss is about.' His disparaging glance swept the woolshed. 'Weddings are all the same,' he told her contemptuously. 'Everyone looks the same; everyone says the same thing. The same tired old rituals every time. The dress, the photographs, the speeches, the bouquet.'

He sneered at the flowers that Lizzy held in her hand, and she pulled them protectively closer to her. 'I love all the wedding traditions,' she said with a defiant look. 'If I ever got married, I'd have the lot!'

'But what's the point?' Tye asked, and Lizzy could practically see his lip curling at the idea of her in a long white dress.

'You can cut all the cakes and toss all the bouquets you want,' he went on, 'but it won't change the fact that when it comes down to it marriage is a transaction like any other, and the moment one party thinks it's not getting its fair share of the deal the whole thing falls apart. Before you know where you are, all the people who forked out for a wedding present are being sent notices about the divorce!'

'You're just a cynic,' Lizzy accused him.

'A realist,' he corrected her.

'Marriage isn't a *transaction*! It's about love and commitment and sharing.'

'You're just a romantic,' mocked Tye.

'Why do people always sneer when they say that?' demanded Lizzy hotly, forgetting that she had accused him in exactly the same tone of voice. 'There's nothing wrong with believing in love!'

Tye shook his head. 'It never fails to amaze me how otherwise intelligent people persist in the starry-eyed belief that a wedding is the beginning of happy-ever-after! Haven't you ever come across the statistics about divorce in those papers you read?'

'Of course I have,' she said with dignity. 'That's why you should wait until you're absolutely sure that you're marrying the right person. And "wait" does seem to be the operative word,' she added, only half joking. 'I'm thirty-three, and I'm still waiting! I should never have agreed to be Ellie's bridesmaid.' She looked glumly down at the flowers. 'You know what they say—three times a bridesmaid, never a bride.'

'Don't despair,' said Tye, irony and something else that she couldn't identify in his voice. 'You caught the bouquet.'

'I don't think it counts if it's thrown straight at you.' Lizzy sighed, and then blushed slightly as she caught Tye's eye. He obviously had her down as a desperate thirty-something. She really must make an effort to sound more positive.

'Anyway,' she hurried on, 'I've decided that I'm not getting married until I know it's going to be perfect, and in the meantime I'm concentrating on my career.'

'Ah, yes.' He smiled sardonically. 'The professional woman. Did you say that you were in PR?'

'Yes. I'm a freelance consultant,' she said grandly, hoping that Tye wouldn't guess that her efforts to establish herself had so far amounted to precisely nothing.

'There can't be much scope for public relations around here,' he commented.

Lizzy shook her head so that the blonde hair bobbed

around her face. 'No, I don't think anyone in Mathison even knows what PR stands for! I live in Perth,' she explained. 'I've only come home for Ellie's wedding, and I'm going back on Monday.'

'I see.' For some reason Tye was studying her with a new kind of interest. 'Are you busy at the moment?'

'I've got several projects in the pipeline,' she said with feigned nonchalance.

Her project for Monday involved buying the paper and scanning it for a job—any job—that would pay her bills and mean that she didn't have to go crawling back to her old boss to ask for her old job back. No need to tell Tye Gibson that, though.

'I don't suppose you know of anyone who might be interested in a…special assignment?' he asked casually.

Lizzy stared at him. 'You've got a job?'

'I guess you could call it that.'

There was a distinctly dry note to his voice, but Lizzy was too excited to notice. Tye Gibson might not be the most popular boss in the world, but there was no doubt that GCS was a hugely prestigious company. If she could put GCS in her portfolio, clients would be queuing up to employ her as a consultant.

'What kind of a job?' she asked, trying desperately not to sound too eager.

Tye hesitated slightly. 'It's highly confidential,' he told her. 'I don't want to give too much away until I'm sure I've got the right person.'

Confidential? That sounded promising. Lizzy moistened her lips. 'As it happens, I've got a window coming up,' she said airily. 'I might be interested.'

The cool grey eyes studied her, and she forced herself to meet his gaze calmly. 'We're talking about an important position,' he said eventually. 'I need somebody with the right instincts.'

Lizzy bridled at his dubious expression. 'I'm completely professional!'

'Professional is easy.' Tye waved a dismissive hand. 'I'm looking for someone who isn't afraid to stand out from the crowd. Someone with ambition. Someone who's prepared to do anything to get the job done.'

'I'm all of those things,' she assured him.

'Are you? I asked around about you earlier, and all anybody would tell me was that you were a nice girl. Now, there's nothing wrong with nice girls, but they don't last long in a competitive commercial situation. I think you're too nice for me,' he told her bluntly.

'Not always.' Lizzy was dismayed. It looked as if the fantastic opportunity that had arisen so unexpectedly was already fading from her grasp. Working for GCS would be the end of all her problems, she thought grimly. She *couldn't* let it go.

'It's my sister's wedding,' she said crisply. 'Of course I'm being nice today, but I'm quite different when I'm at work.'

Tye looked unconvinced. 'I haven't got time to deal with tears and tantrums and wounded feelings,' he warned her. 'I've only got time for results. Are you telling me that you're hard-nosed enough to play ball with me?'

'I know I am,' said Lizzy with a show of confidence that effectively disguised her inner qualms. She wasn't going to back down now. She *needed* that job. 'What do I have to do to convince you?'

Tye didn't answer immediately. He considered the

matter, looking around the woolshed before his gaze came back to settle speculatively on Lizzy's face.

'I'll do anything,' she said rashly.

'OK,' said Tye. 'Kiss me.'

CHAPTER TWO

'*KISS* you?' Lizzy flushed in embarrassment as she heard her voice rise to a squeak, and she cleared her throat quickly.

'Why should I do that?' That was better. Deeper, steadier, just a touch of amusement to show that she recognised that he was joking. *Much* more like the sophisticated PR consultant she was supposed to be.

'You said that you would do anything,' Tye pointed out.

Without quite knowing why, Lizzy's assurance began to trickle away, and she eyed him uneasily. 'Well, I know I did, but...'

'Are you trying to tell me that you're *not* prepared to do anything?'

'You're not serious!'

'Don't I look serious?'

He did. Absolutely serious.

Lizzy swallowed. 'Do you interview all your prospective employees like this?'

'Only those with the potential to fulfil a very special role.' Tye's face was still perfectly straight, but Lizzy seized on the glimmer of amusement she could see in the grey eyes.

'You *are* joking!'

'No, I'm not,' he said. 'You asked what you could do to convince me that it was worth giving you a chance, and I've told you. You can kiss me.'

'But how can you possibly tell anything about my PR

21

skills from a kiss?' Lizzy objected, trying to ignore the way her heart was racketing around her chest at the mere thought of kissing him.

'I'm not interested in your skills,' said Tye. 'I want to know whether you're the kind of person who's prepared to stand out from the crowd—and I don't just mean by wearing ridiculous shoes. Look around you, Lizzy,' he went on, nodding his head in the direction of the other guests. 'See how many people are watching us while trying not to make it obvious. They don't like the fact that you're talking to me.'

It was true. Lizzy, following his glance, noticed how friends that she had known for years averted their eyes while others were eyeing her covertly. It was an uncomfortable feeling, and she turned back to Tye, an uncharacteristic frown in her blue eyes.

OK, so he wasn't the most charming man in the world, and his reputation certainly didn't bear close scrutiny, but he wasn't *that* bad. Lizzy wouldn't go so far as to say that she liked him. He was cold and callous, and he had made little attempt to conceal his contempt for her family and friends, but there was something intriguing about him, something that stimulated and provoked and disconcerted her all at the same time.

'I'm not welcome here,' Tye was saying, not sounding at all bothered by the fact. 'No one has been prepared to come right out and say it, but it's obvious. I don't belong here, and if I'd given them the slightest excuse there would have been plenty of people more than happy to throw me out. It's been bad enough for them to see you standing here with me all this time. How do you think they'd react if you kissed me?'

Lizzy tried to picture the scene, but although she could imagine kissing Tye with startling clarity, somehow she couldn't get past that to visualise the reactions of anyone watching.

'You'd be breaking ranks big time,' Tye answered for her. 'You'd be saying you didn't care what anyone thought, that you'd do whatever it took to get what you want.' He looked into Lizzy's face, a faint smile on his lips as doubt wrestled with determination to prove herself in the blue eyes. 'And *that's* the kind of person I'm looking for,' he said.

'And if I don't want to break ranks?'

Tye shrugged carelessly. 'You walk away. I leave. I find someone else.'

He might at least sound as if he cared one way or another, thought Lizzy with something suspiciously close to petulance. She looked away from him, edgily running a finger around the base of her glass.

She had always prided herself on her refusal to fit the mould. As a young girl she had grumbled endlessly about the old-fashioned attitudes of her parents and their friends. The district might cover vast distances but it had a distinctly small town mentality.

Lizzy hadn't been able to wait to leave home for the city. She thought of herself as cosmopolitan, and whenever she came home she made a point of looking as stylish as possible. Her transformation into city girl was treated as something of a standing joke in the community, and Lizzy played up to it. She knew that the teasing was affectionate, and she liked the fact that they thought of her as unconventional.

You'd be saying you didn't care what anyone thought. Tye had issued a challenge, and she longed to take it up, but deep down Lizzy knew that she *did* care. These people were her family and friends. She might not choose to live in the outback, but that didn't mean she wanted to shock or offend them unnecessarily. When it came down to it, Lizzy just wanted everyone to like her.

There would be uproar if she kissed Tye Gibson, and in spite of her assertion of confidence Lizzy quailed inwardly at the thought.

'I can hardly fling myself into your arms in the middle of my sister's wedding,' she prevaricated, unaware that her thoughts were written clearly in her expressive face. 'It would cause a scene. While it might prove your point, I'm not prepared to do anything to spoil her day. It wouldn't be fair.'

Tye looked faintly bored by her dithering. 'I wasn't thinking of a passionate clinch,' he said with a sardonic look. 'I know you're much too *nice* a girl to go in for anything like that!'

'Oh.'

Lizzy wasn't sure she liked the way he'd said that word 'nice'. It wasn't that she wanted to kiss him—God forbid!—but she didn't want to be the kind of girl who didn't dare either. She stood feeling foolish, unable to decide whether she was relieved or offended at Tye's lack of interest in being kissed by her.

'What *were* you thinking of?' she asked him uncertainly.

'More along the lines of a peck on the cheek,' said Tye, lifting his brows in a way that made Lizzy feel ridiculous for having thought that he could possibly mean anything else. 'A quick kiss to say goodbye, that's all.'

'Oh,' said Lizzy again.

She bit her lip. Between the crowds, she caught a glimpse of her parents, greeting friends on the other side of the woolshed. They wouldn't like her kissing Tye at all, and nor would anyone else.

Perhaps no one would notice. It would be dark by then and the party would be well away. Everyone would be too busy enjoying themselves to wonder what she was doing with Tye Gibson, and anyway, it would only take a second.

And it would be worth it. *A very special role*, wasn't that what Tye had called it? Quite apart from what it would do for her CV, an important job with a company like GCS was bound to be lucrative, Lizzy calculated.

It was all very well not wanting to upset anybody, but the hard fact was that she needed the money. Since Stephen had moved out she had had all the bills to pay, and Ellie's wedding had proved expensive, too, what with flying backwards and forwards between Perth and Mathison, buying presents and searching out the perfect bridesmaid's dress.

Not to mention the shoes.

Lizzy contemplated the champagne in her glass with an inward grimace at the thought of her credit card bill. Face it, her only other choice was to get a bar job of some kind to tide her over. It wasn't that she hadn't done it before, but it certainly wasn't what she had planned to be doing at thirty-three, and the prospect was humiliating when she thought about how she had boasted about her grand new career.

She could ask her parents for help, but it wouldn't be fair right now when they had all the expense of Ellie's wedding to cope with. No, Lizzy decided, she wouldn't go to them. It was her own fault that she had given up a perfectly good job, and it was up to her to find a way out of her financial problems.

She could settle for a bar job.

Or she could kiss Tye Gibson.

A choice between scraping together enough money to

pay the bills and seizing the opportunity of an important job with a prestigious organisation that could relaunch her career. Why was she even hesitating? Lizzy wondered.

Tye had been watching the conflicting emotions flitting across her face, but now he looked ostentatiously at his watch and put down his glass. 'I might as well go,' he said.

'What, now?' Lizzy regarded him with dismay. She had thought that she would have the rest of the evening to build up courage.

'No point in hanging around,' said Tye. 'I've done what I came to do. I thought it would be interesting to see if things had changed round here, but obviously they haven't.' The grey eyes gleamed with mockery as he looked at Lizzy. 'Shall I see myself out, or are you coming?'

How hard could it be? It was ridiculous to make such a fuss about a tiny kiss. All she had to do was walk across the woolshed with him, say goodbye and press her cheek to his.

Piece of cake.

Lizzy put down her glass. 'I'll come with you,' she said.

Something flickered in Tye's eyes, and was gone. 'Good,' was all he said.

Turning, he headed across the middle of the woolshed floor to the wide wooden doors that stood open to the night. No creeping round the edges for Tye Gibson, thought Lizzy with a mixture of exasperation and admiration as she hurried to keep up with him. He went straight for what he wanted, and to hell with anyone who got in his way.

He walked with the long, deliberate stride of a man

used to walking alone, appearing not to notice the almost
tangible hostility of the crowd, or the way it parted uneasily before his ruthless self-assurance. Struggling to
keep up with him in her frivolous shoes, Lizzy was very
conscious of the eyes following her. So much for not
being noticed. They might as well have had a brass band
and ticker tape.

A murmuring rose behind them as the guests closed
back into their groups, but she didn't hear. Tye had
paused at the doors and was waiting for her to catch up.
Lizzy told herself that her sudden breathlessness was due
to hurrying on unsteady heels, and nothing whatsoever
to do with the fact that any moment now she was going
to kiss him.

Outside, it was already dark. Two more steps would
have taken them into the shadows, but he had stopped
deliberately in the doorway so that they were framed
against the darkness in the brightness of the light that
shone directly above their heads. It was like being on
stage.

'I'll say goodbye,' said Tye, and held out his hand.
His face was quite straight, but the startlingly light eyes
glinted with a mocking challenge.

He thought that she would lose her nerve, Lizzy realised, and it was enough to bring her chin up. This was
her chance to prove herself.

She took his outstretched hand. 'Goodbye,' she said,
surprised at how steady her voice sounded.

The press of his palm was cool and firm, and as his
fingers closed around hers she felt something uncurl
alarmingly inside her, but she made herself look directly
into his eyes, her own very blue and sparkling with defiance.

'It was nice to meet you,' she went on deliberately,

and without releasing her grip she brought her other hand up to rest against his chest.

She could feel the power of his body through his jacket. It seemed to reverberate through her palm, tingling along her arm and deep into the core of her being, and she had a sudden, vivid sense that time had slowed while her senses simultaneously speeded up. She was acutely aware of the texture of the material beneath her hand, of Tye's fingers imprisoning hers, of the sound of her own heart thudding in her ears.

Lizzy was a tall girl, but Tye was taller still, and when he made no effort to bend his head she had to lift herself onto her toes to bring her face close to his, balancing herself by spreading her hand against his chest. She pressed her cheek against Tye's cool skin, feeling its roughness, breathing in his clean, masculine smell, grazing it with her lips, shivering at the sensation.

Everything seemed to be happening hazily, as if in slow motion. Lizzy had forgotten their audience, but she hadn't forgotten what she was doing, and when she felt Tye's fingers begin to loosen their grip she tightened her hold. If she was making a point, she might as well make it properly. She would show Tye just how willing she was to stand out from the crowd!

Tye tensed questioningly as her hand slid up from his chest to his shoulder, and she turned her head. For a fleeting moment blue eyes looked into grey, and then Lizzy smiled, lowering her lashes, and all at once it seemed perfectly natural to touch her mouth to his.

She was prepared for his lips to feel as cold and unyielding as the rest of him, but they weren't like that at all. They were firm, yes, but they were *warm*, warm and inviting and exciting, and Lizzy was jarred by a deep, instinctive sense of rightness that was as undeniable as it was disturbing.

Perturbed by the feeling, she would have pulled away if Tye hadn't chosen that exact moment to put his free arm around her and lift her hard against him. Lizzy found herself pinioned between the massive solidity of his body and the steel strength of his arm, and she felt at once helpless and disconcertingly secure.

His mouth returned the pressure of hers for a long, giddying moment, his lips searingly persuasive, and his hand burning through the silky dress onto her skin—the briefest of touches, but enough to galvanise Lizzy's senses in a single, incandescent instant so electric that she gasped.

It was enough to break the kiss. Tye's arm fell, his hand released hers, and Lizzy was left, dizzy and disorientated, somehow managing to stand upright on legs that twitched and trembled with a life of their own. The blue eyes were dazed, and she blinked furiously to clear her head.

What had happened? One second she had been coolly determined to impress him, and the next…oh, the next there had been that scorching whoosh of sensation, thrilling and terrifying at the same time. Lizzy couldn't have even said how long it lasted. She knew only that it had been long enough to jolt the world out of its usual orbit and that nothing was quite the same as it had been before.

Shaken, she focused at last on her hand. It was clutching Tye's shoulder, crumpling his jacket between her fingers, and the belated recognition that she was still clinging to him was enough to make Lizzy snatch it away, although she could have done with the support.

She had kissed him because she needed a job, not a shoulder to lean on. *Remember?*

'Will—?' She stopped, horrified by the huskiness of her voice. 'Will you consider me now?' she managed croakily after having to clear her throat humiliatingly a couple of times.

'I certainly will,' said Tye, and then he demolished all Lizzy's desperate attempts to pull herself together by smiling.

He had smiled at her before, but his smiles had been mocking at best. This smile was different. It softened the grim lines of his face and warmed the cool eyes with a blithe charm that was as devastating as it was unexpected, and Lizzy's heart did a peculiar somersault that left her even more breathless than she had been before. It was as if she had blinked to find someone completely different standing before her.

'Wh—wh—when...?' she stammered, trying to ask him about the interview, but her tongue kept sticking to the roof of her mouth, so thick and unwieldy that she couldn't get the words out.

Tye seemed to understand. Reaching into his inside pocket, he pulled out a business card and offered it to Lizzy, who took it with nerveless fingers.

'Give me a call,' he said, and turned to walk out of the woolshed and away into the starry outback night, leaving Lizzy to stare after him, his card clutched unread in her hand.

Five to eight. Lizzy looked at her watch for the umpteenth time, and wondered if it was too late to change her shoes.

She had been pleased with her reflection when she left her room. Having dithered for ages about what she should wear, Lizzy had settled at length on a plain shift dress which was flattering without being too revealing. It was very simply cut, relying on the vibrant turquoise colour and the softness of the material for its effect. Lizzy thought it made her look stylish and professional, without making it seem as if she had tried too hard to impress Tye.

Maybe it was a bit shorter than she would normally wear to an interview, but then most interviews didn't involve being flown to Sydney and collected from the airport by limousine, or being put up in a hotel so luxurious her eyes had popped when she saw the room.

It had taken Lizzy ages to pluck up the courage to ring Tye on the Monday after Ellie's wedding. She'd sat by the phone, tapping his card against her teeth, wishing she could put that kiss from her mind and feeling ridiculously, *pathetically* nervous at the idea of seeing him again. Even the thought of his voice at the other end of the phone had been enough to set the nerves jittering and jangling underneath her skin.

What had been the point of going through all that to get his number if she wasn't even going to call him? Lizzy had asked herself sternly. Chances were that Tye would simply put her in touch with the personnel department and she would never have anything else to do with him.

She had to pay for those shoes somehow, didn't she?

And after all that, when she'd finally dialled the number, she'd got not Tye but his icily efficient assistant, who had told her that she would make arrangements for Lizzy to fly to Sydney. Mr Gibson, she'd said, would see her for dinner the following Friday at eight o'clock. It seemed a funny time for an interview, but Lizzy had been too intimidated by the PA's manner to question her further.

Her spirits had risen on the flight over to Sydney. A first-class ticket, limousine service from the airport, a luxurious suite in a top-class hotel... Tye must have been serious about it being an important job. Lizzy congratulated herself on having had the courage to kiss him. It had been awkward afterwards, to say the least, but clearly it had been worth it.

To celebrate, Lizzy had taken herself shopping as soon as she'd arrived in Sydney, and had found a pair of shoes so perfect for her dress that she hadn't been able to resist buying them to wear instead of the elegant black ones that she had brought with her. Now, sitting beside an elaborate fountain in the lobby as she waited for Tye to arrive, Lizzy wondered if they had been such a good idea.

They *were* beautiful, just the right colour and decorated with mock peacock feathers fixed into place by a glass jewel, but perhaps they were, after all, a bit much?

Everybody else in the hotel was dressed so discreetly you just knew their clothes had cost a fortune, and Lizzy had seen one or two glances at her shoes, usually followed by disparagingly raised eyebrows. The gesture reminded her sharply of Tye.

He would be here any minute. Lizzy looked at her watch again, trying to ignore the churning sense of anticipation and nerves. Beside her, the water trickled into the fountain in a way that was meant to be soothing but instead was having the opposite effect. She crossed her legs, then uncrossed them, drummed her fingers on the edge of her seat, resisted the urge to check her make-up.

Really, she was being ridiculous! Lizzy sat upright.

This was an interview, not a date. She would be fine. All she had to do was be cool and professional, and let Tye know that as far as she was concerned the kiss had been no more than a mildly unusual interviewing technique.

'Cool...professional...' she muttered to herself, only to find her eyes drawn back to her shoes.

No, they weren't the right image! She would have to go and change. If she hurried, she could get up to her room and back before he arrived.

Jumping to her feet, Lizzy turned towards the lifts, but she had only taken three steps before the glass doors hissed open and Tye strode into the lobby.

The air leaked out of Lizzy's lungs at the sight of him, and she stopped dead, conscious of a sense of recognition so sharp that it was almost a shock. It wasn't that she hadn't expected to recognise Tye, it was just that she hadn't been prepared for him to seem quite so...*familiar*. It was as if she had always known that dark, guarded face, the watchful eyes, that air of barely leashed power.

Pausing in the middle of the lobby, Tye let his piercing gaze sweep round until he found Lizzy. Skewered by his eyes, she could only stand frozen by the fountain, her heart beating frantically in her throat as he came towards her.

'Hi!' She smiled nervously, wincing inwardly as she heard her own voice. Cool and professional? Yeah, *sure*!

Clearing her throat, Lizzy held out her hand. 'Thank you for seeing me.'

An improvement. Composed, competent, in control. Well, fairly.

There was an odd look in Tye's eyes as he inspected her, subjecting her to an intense but strangely impersonal scrutiny. His gaze travelled from the soft mass of blonde hair framing her face, with its tilting blue eyes and wide, humorous mouth, skimming over the vivid dress and down the long, slender legs, ending at the shoes with their jaunty feathers and gaudy jewels.

One corner of his mouth quirked, and he lifted his eyes to Lizzy's. 'It's a pleasure,' he said.

He took her hand, and the moment his fingers closed around hers Lizzy felt her composure wobble. His clasp was warm and firm, and the touch of his palm sent little tingles down her arm. All he had to do was shake her hand and she was drowning in giddying sensation, as if they'd kissed all over again. It wasn't fair.

'You're very formal,' said Tye, and his eyes glinted. 'We kissed last time we met,' he reminded her.

As if she would have forgotten. As if she couldn't still feel his jacket beneath her fingers, his lips on hers, the deep, dangerous twist of excitement. As if she hadn't relived every second of that kiss and how it had felt as his arm came round her like an iron bar and lifted her effortlessly against him.

Lizzy moistened her lips surreptitiously. 'That was just because I wanted an interview,' she said, raising her voice above the bumping and thumping of her heart.

She wished he would let her hand go, but when she tried to pull it away Tye's grip tightened. 'It worked,' he said, a glimmer of amusement in his eyes as he drew her inexorably towards him, 'but this time let's kiss because we're pleased to see each other.'

It was just like the wedding, only this time it was Tye who made the first move, Tye whose lips brushed the edge of her mouth and lingered against her cheek.

To anyone watching it must have seemed the coolest of kisses, but Lizzy's senses were drumming beneath her skin, preternaturally alert to the smell of his hair, to the touch of his lips, to the feel of his cool, masculine skin, and she was suddenly overwhelmed by an inexplicable urge to lean into him, to turn her head and let their mouths meet, so that they could kiss just as they had kissed before.

For one dizzying moment she was sure that Tye was going to do just that, and she closed her eyes, bracing herself against the terrifying jolt of response, but after the tiniest of hesitations Tye lifted his head and let her go.

A polite kiss, a mere grazing of cheeks; that was all it had been. Lizzy's eyes snapped open and her cheeks burned with a mixture of disappointment and fury at her own foolishness in thinking it might have been anything else.

Had Tye guessed how close she had come to making a complete idiot of herself? Lizzy slid a glance at him from under her lashes, but his expression was impossible to read. He looked as sardonic and indifferent as ever, she thought with a spurt of resentment. If the touch of their cheeks had set *his* senses spinning, he was giving absolutely no sign of it.

'Come,' said Tye, taking her arm. 'We'll have a drink before we go.'

He steered her towards a bar that was discreetly hidden behind lush potted palms, and Lizzy, burningly aware of the touch of his hand against her bare arm, let herself be led. Her legs felt ridiculously unsteady and she was glad to sink down into one of the plush armchairs.

A barman materialised in response to Tye's barely lifted finger. 'Champagne,' ordered Tye without even looking at him.

'Certainly, sir.'

'Champagne?' Lizzy made an enormous effort to pull herself together. Cool and professional, right?

Right.

'What are we celebrating?' she asked, hoping that she sounded like the kind of person who was only ever interviewed over a glass of champagne.

'The fact that you came.'

Lizzy stared at him. She wasn't sure what she had been expecting him to say. Perhaps a billion-dollar deal closed, or a rival company crushed. Anything except what he *had* said.

Belatedly aware that her jaw was hanging open, Lizzy snapped her mouth shut. 'Did you think that I wouldn't?' she asked cautiously.

Tye seemed to consider the matter. 'I wasn't sure,' he said eventually.

'I wouldn't have kissed you if I hadn't really wanted you to consider me for the job,' Lizzy pointed out, and was then afraid that it might seem as if she was protesting just a little too much.

'True.' Tye was unperturbed by her unflattering motives. 'But I did wonder if you might have changed your mind once I'd left. There must have been plenty of people there trying to persuade you that it would be a terrible mistake to have anything to do with me. Or are you going to tell me that nobody noticed the affectionate farewell you gave me?'

'They noticed all right,' said Lizzy with feeling, remembering the moment when she had turned from the woolshed doors to face the avid or outraged stares. 'Mum wasn't very pleased.'

That was understatement of the year. Her mother

hadn't actually seen the kiss, but she had heard plenty about it and she had been appalled.

'It was bad enough him turning up at the wedding at all, without you kissing him! What on earth possessed you to make such an exhibition of yourself?'

'I felt sorry for him,' Lizzy had said.

She had been strangely reluctant to admit the truth about that kiss. If she'd told her mother that she had had to kiss Tye to get him to consider her for a job, it would only have added to his reputation, and that was bad enough as it was. Lizzy couldn't think of any good reason why Tye's reputation should matter to her; she just knew that she didn't want to be responsible for blackening it any further.

'Sorry for Tye Gibson? You must be the first person ever to feel *that*!'

That was probably true, Lizzy had thought wryly. It wasn't easy to pity a man like Tye. He was too tough, too competent, too indifferent to what people thought of him.

'He wasn't exactly made to feel welcome,' she'd tried to explain to her mother. 'I felt as if I ought to make an effort to talk to him. We did invite him, after all.'

'That was your father's fault,' her mother had grumbled. 'Why did he come, anyway? He didn't talk to anyone except you.'

'Maybe that's because nobody except me bothered to talk to *him*,' Lizzy had said with a shade of defiance, even as she'd wondered what on earth she was doing defending Tye Gibson.

'Nobody except you would have thought they had to fling themselves into his arms just to be polite!' her mother had retorted, clearly baffled by Lizzy's behaviour. 'It's absolutely typical of you, Lizzy! You always go too far!'

Lizzy had given up then. She did feel a little guilty about having caused a scene at Ellie's wedding, but it wasn't as if she had hurt anyone's feelings. And she certainly didn't feel guilty enough to give up her best chance yet of a real job.

Muttering vaguely about the possibility of a job in Sydney as she'd left, Lizzy had prudently kept Tye Gibson's name out of it. Her mother would have a fit when she heard, but Lizzy would deal with that when—if—she got the job.

'She doesn't approve of me?' Tye broke into her thoughts. It was more of a statement than a question.

Her mother's words rang in Lizzy's ears: 'That Tye Gibson is no good! He never was and he never will be! He broke his poor father's heart, Lizzy, and he'll break a lot more hearts before he's finished, you mark my words. Don't you have anything to do with him!'

'Well...not really,' she said cautiously.

'Good,' he said coolly. 'I have to confess when I met you at your sister's wedding I thought you would be too nice. I had you down as the kind of person who has to be liked, but if you're prepared to meet me again in the face of family disapproval, that means you've got what it takes after all.'

Lizzy couldn't imagine anyone else being pleased to hear that they were thoroughly disliked. 'It means I need a job,' she told him honestly.

'I know.' Tye leant forward and looked straight into her puzzled blue eyes. 'I've got a feeling that it also means you could be *just* the girl I'm looking for!'

CHAPTER THREE

THE look in his eyes was making Lizzy's heart pound, and she could feel herself blushing. Don't be an idiot, she told herself fiercely. He's talking about a *job*. He's not interested in you.

'Great,' she said with an unconvincing smile.

To her relief, the barman arrived just then with an ice bucket. He set it down on the table between Tye and Lizzy, and her eyes widened at the label on the bottle as he drew it from the ice and eased out the cork with a subtle, extremely expensive pop. If this was the champagne Tye was used to drinking, it was no wonder he had turned up his nose at what had been served at Ellie's wedding!

Tye waited until the barman had poured two glasses, settled the bottle back on the ice and disappeared as noiselessly as he had arrived. He leant forward and picked up his glass, chinking it against Lizzy's.

'Here's to a successful partnership!' he said.

Partnership? Did he say *partnership*? Lizzy stared at him. 'You mean I've got the job?' she asked incredulously.

'If you want it,' said Tye carefully.

Did she want it? Did a drowning man want a lifebelt? Lizzy laughed.

'I want it,' she assured him gaily. 'Oh, this is fantastic! *Thank you!*' She beamed at him as they chinked glasses again, her blue eyes sparkling with delight. 'I can't tell you what a relief it is,' she babbled on, all

39

smiles as she settled back into her chair, able to relax at last. 'I was beginning to wonder if I'd ever find another job!'

To think that she had been contemplating that advert for a waitress in the local café, and now here she was being offered a job with GCS! Lizzy's mind raced ahead to the future. Working for such an international company, there were bound to be opportunities for travel, weren't there? Lizzy pictured herself armed with a battery of mobile phones and an electronic organiser, jumping on and off planes, dashing around New York and... And what?

Her careering fantasy screeched to a halt as she realised that she still had no idea at all of what the job entailed. 'Er...what exactly *is* this special project you want me for?' she asked Tye.

He hesitated. 'It's complicated,' he said at last. 'And very sensitive. I don't want to say any more until I'm sure that I can trust you.'

Lizzy's rocketing spirits collapsed. 'You mean, you might not want me after all?' she said, unable to keep the disappointment from her voice. Surely he had said that the job was hers if she wanted it?

Tye looked at her, the corners of his mouth lifting in a slight smile. 'Oh, no, I want you all right,' he said. 'But you might change your mind when you know what's involved, and I don't want to explain that just yet. Do you mind?'

Lizzy didn't think that she was in any position to mind. 'Well, no, of course not,' she said, completely mystified.

What on earth was he going to ask her to do? The obvious suspicion flickered across her mind, only to be dismissed. A man like Tye didn't need to pay women to sleep with him, and anyway, judging by those whose names had been linked with his in the gossip columns, she wasn't exactly his type. He seemed to like his women dark and exotic, and she could hardly be described as either. She was too blonde, too normal.

Too *nice*.

Lizzy looked at the tiny bubbles drifting lazily upwards in her glass and sighed.

'I'm sorry if it seems unreasonable,' said Tye, misinterpreting her expression, 'but you'll understand later why I don't want to put all my cards on the table right now.'

'Can't you say *anything* about it?' Lizzy pleaded. 'At least tell me if it's a PR job!'

'I think you could say that,' he conceded.

'Doesn't GCS have a PR department already?'

Tye frowned down into his champagne. 'This isn't to do with GCS,' he said, and then lifted his eyes to meet Lizzy's confused blue gaze. 'It's to do with me.'

'I see,' she said, although she didn't.

'Look,' he said, raking a hand through his dark hair in a gesture of frustration, 'let's start again, shall we? We'll treat this as an ordinary interview, and I'll explain everything later.'

'All right,' said Lizzy in some relief. She knew where she was with an interview. 'Not that most ordinary interviews are conducted over champagne like this!' she couldn't resist adding with a glance at the bottle.

Tye shrugged. It was clearly your common-or-garden everyday champagne as far as he was concerned. 'I thought if we had a drink together, and dinner, it would be a good way to find out more about you,' he said with an edge of impatience. 'We can go back to the office and sit on either side of a desk if you'd prefer.'

'No, no, this is fine!' said Lizzy hastily. She put her glass on the table, sat upright, smoothed her dress down over her knees and looked expectantly at Tye. 'Where do you want me to begin? With my last job?'

'No.' Tye waved her precious work experience aside. 'I'm more interested in your personal background.'

'But you know all that,' she objected.

'Do I? I know you grew up in the outback but live in the city. I know that you're very sociable, and that you have a very…' He paused, searching for the right word. 'A very *individual* taste in shoes,' he decided. 'But that's about it. There must be more to you than that.'

God, yes, there must, thought Lizzy, racking her brains to think of something else to convince him that she was really a complex and interesting personality. A sociable, city-dwelling shoe-lover. All true, but it did make her sound a bit superficial.

'I like reading,' she said lamely, although she really preferred a good movie, or an afternoon's shopping.

She could see from Tye's face that he was not impressed. 'Well, what else do you want to know?' she asked crossly.

'How about why a woman with your personality and apparent ability is so desperate for a job that she's prepared to take on an assignment without even knowing what it is or what she'll have to do?' Tye suggested in a dry voice.

'It was my own fault,' Lizzy admitted after a long pause. She might as well tell him. 'It took me ages to decide what I wanted to do. I tried all sorts of jobs, but eventually I ended up in PR, and it was perfect for me. I loved the parties and the organisation and the…the *buzz*.'

She waved her hands to try and illustrate the excitement of those heady days. 'I managed to get a job with one of the top agencies in Perth, and for a while everything was fine. It was more than fine, actually. I had a great job, a fantastic social life, a wonderful boyfriend. We got engaged, had a wild party.' She smiled a little sadly. 'I thought I had it all.'

'So what happened?' asked Tye, a faint sneer in his voice. 'Did your wonderful boyfriend turn out to be not so wonderful after all?'

'No, nothing like that.' Lizzy shook her head. The light gleamed on her blonde hair as she leant forward to pick up her glass and sipped her champagne as she tried to think how to explain to someone as cynical as Tye what had prompted her to do what she had done.

'An old friend of mine got married,' she said at last. 'I went up for the wedding, and seeing Gray and Clare together...well, I guess it made me realise what I was missing. I don't really know how to explain it,' she went on, looking at Tye's sceptical expression. 'I enjoy my life, but theirs was somehow more intense, more vivid.

'I realised that I was in a rut, not just professionally but emotionally. Stephen was—is—wonderful, but we didn't have what Clare and Gray have. We'd been living together for about a year, and we'd sort of drifted into the idea of getting married. We were good friends, comfortable together, and there wasn't anyone else for either of us. It seemed like a good idea at the time, but when I compared our relationship to Gray and Clare's, I knew that it wasn't enough.'

Lizzy's head was bent as she told her story, apparently absorbed in the invisible patterns she was tracing on the arm of the chair, but she looked up then to see if Tye was listening. 'When I went home, I told Stephen I wouldn't marry him.'

'It was a bit hard on him, wasn't it?' Tye had been listening all right, but he obviously wasn't impressed. His grey eyes were alert and very cool.

'Stephen didn't mind.' Lizzy went back to her patterns, remembering how they had talked that night. An angry scene would have been awful, but at least it would have meant that Stephen had cared enough about her to try and make her change her mind. Instead it had all been very civilised. He had listened and agreed that breaking their engagement would be for the best.

'I think he was quite relieved really,' she went on. It had been just the same with Gray all those years ago. 'I seem to be the kind of woman men just want to be friends with,' she sighed.

Tye looked at her across the table. She might sound despondent, but it was hard for her to look glum. There was an irrepressibly merry curve to her mouth, and the laughter lines starring the corners of her deep blue eyes with their tilting lashes gave her expression a warmth and a humour that was much more appealing than mere beauty.

His gaze dropped to her bare shoulders. Her creamy skin was dusted with a golden summer glow. It shadowed invitingly into her cleavage and in the hollow at the base of her throat. Aware of his eyes, Lizzy lifted her hand and pushed the silky mass of hair away from her face in an unconsciously nervous gesture, but it wouldn't stay behind her ears and fell forward again, swinging softly against her cheek.

'I wouldn't say that,' he said, and he smiled a wickedly attractive smile that sent the colour surging into Lizzy's cheeks.

How old did you have to be before you stopped blushing when a man looked at you? Lizzy wondered in de-

spair. Avoiding his gaze, she took a defiant gulp of
champagne and set her glass back on the table with a
sharp click.

'Yes, well, anyway,' she said with a tiny cough to
clear her throat. 'Once I'd sorted things out with Stephen
I felt much better, but I knew I had to do the same with
work. I'd been at the agency too long and I was getting
stale. I went in the next day and handed in my resig-
nation in a grand gesture. I told them I needed a new
challenge and that I was going to set up on my own as
a freelance consultant.'

'And did you?'

'I tried, but it was hopeless. There wasn't enough
work to go round as it was, and I couldn't compete with
the agencies. I must have trudged round every office in
Perth looking for a client, but I wasn't getting anywhere.
I was about to give in when I met you and you mentioned this job. It's my last chance to make it on my
own.'

'I'm beginning to see why you were so keen to be
considered,' said Tye.

Lizzy's colour deepened. He hadn't said anything, but
she knew that he was thinking about the way she had
kissed him at the wedding, and she tilted her chin. It
wouldn't do any harm for him to realise that she had
only kissed him like that because she had been desperate.

'It's been months now since I had a regular income,'
she told him. 'I know I should be able to manage, but
I'm not very good at economising, and I'm up to my
ears in debt.' She sighed. 'I went about things all wrong;
I know that now. I should have waited until I'd decided
exactly what I was going to do and had my financial
situation sorted out instead of just chucking in a really

good job and then wondering how I was going to get by.'

'I don't agree,' said Tye to her surprise.

Lizzy had been prepared for him to pour scorn on her, and his unexpected support took her aback. She eyed him a little warily, wondering if he was being sarcastic.

'I bet you'd never do anything that stupid!'

'I believe in going all out for what you want,' he said coolly, 'and you don't get what you want without taking risks. Do you think I'd have got where I am today if I'd played safe? Twenty years ago I left home with nothing. I worked my way to Sydney and found myself a job and somewhere to live. Those aren't things you take for granted when you've had to survive without either, but when I had an idea I took a chance and gambled everything on it.'

He didn't sound triumphant about it, merely matter-of-fact, and Lizzy looked at him curiously, trying to imagine him as a young man, finding his way in the city, alone and homeless. From that unpromising beginning, he had built up an empire, a vast conglomerate that stretched around the world and had become a watchword for quality and innovation. It made her own idea of a challenge seem pretty pathetic.

'All you need is ambition,' said Tye, 'and if you want it badly enough you can get there. You must have an ambition, don't you?'

Did she? Lizzy considered the matter. 'I'd like to do well at my job, of course, but I don't have any burning desire to succeed. As long as it's interesting and I've got enough to live on, I don't mind. My ambitions aren't that focused. What I'd really like is marriage, a family of my own, the usual. I just want to be happy.'

Tye didn't quite sneer, but there was something very

scornful about the way he reached for the champagne bottle and topped up Lizzy's glass.

'What about you?' she asked abruptly.

'Me?'

'What are your ambitions, or have you achieved them all?'

'No,' said Tye, replacing the bottle carefully in the ice, so that Lizzy couldn't read his expression. 'I've still got one.'

'What is it?'

'To live at Barra Creek.'

Lizzy froze with her glass halfway to her lips. 'Live at Barra Creek?' she echoed in astonishment. 'Whatever for?'

'Just to be there,' said Tye simply.

If he had confessed to an ambition to tap dance his way across the Simpson Desert, wearing only a pink tutu and top hat with corks dangling from it, Lizzy would not have thought it more bizarre. She put her glass down without drinking and stared at him.

'You can't run a company the size of GCS from a cattle station in the outback!'

'Yes, I can,' Tye contradicted her. 'I don't run GCS on a day-to-day basis anyway. I've got highly paid directors to do that for me. All I need to do is to keep in contact, and I can do that from anywhere. We've got the technology now—e-mail, telephone, video links, fax. There's no reason why Barra shouldn't be just as effective a base as an office here in Sydney.'

'But why would you want to?' asked Lizzy, uncomprehending. 'There's nothing there! Think of the places you could base yourself—New York, Tokyo, London, Paris, Rio...' She threw her arms in the air as if she had tossed the world at his feet. 'You're so rich, you can go anywhere, do anything you want. I can't *believe* that you would give up all that and go and live in the outback!'

'Your family do,' Tye pointed out.

'Yes, but that's all they know. They're used to eating beef, beef and more beef, and not having the option of popping out to eat Vietnamese or Thai or Greek if they feel like it. They're not used to the buzz of a city the way you must be. I mean, the bush is beautiful,' Lizzy conceded, 'but it's so quiet and nothing ever happens! There are no restaurants, no shops, no nightlife, no *people*, nothing. Just a lot of scrub and a few cattle.'

'So if this job involved spending time in the outback, you wouldn't want to do it?'

The question caught her off balance. She had forgotten the job for a while there in her amazement at Tye's announcement. She couldn't imagine why he would need her PR skills if he was going to bury himself in the outback. He could have told her that a bit sooner, Lizzy reflected with a tinge of resentment. Now she was going to have to backtrack fast!

'It's not that I don't like the bush,' she assured him. 'I was up there for a month not so long ago, helping to look after a baby on a friend's station, and that was fine. I love going home and seeing my family, too, but after a while I start to pine for the city. I don't mind helping out, but there's a limit to how excited I can get about putting a mob of cattle through the yards, and it's not even as if you get a break. You can't slip out to a café for a quick cappuccino when it's an hour to the nearest sealed road.'

She caught herself up hastily. She didn't want to sound like a whinger. 'But, of course, it would be different working for you. I'd have a job of my own to do—and I don't imagine you'd be going to all this trouble if you just wanted help castrating a few calves?'

'No.' Tye smiled faintly. 'I don't want you to do that.'

'Well, then, I'm sure it won't be a problem,' said Lizzy. 'Frankly, I'm not in a position to pick and choose locations. If the outback is where the job is, that's where I'll go.'

So much for dashing frantically around Manhattan, she thought glumly. How was it that she always seemed to end up back in the bush? Still, it wouldn't be for ever, she consoled herself. Tye had called it a special assignment. He probably wouldn't need her for more than a couple of months.

It was hard to know whether she had convinced him or not. Tye seemed preoccupied. He was leaning forward, apparently absorbed in moving his glass around the low table between them. His head was lowered, giving Lizzy a foreshortened view of his face. She could see his hair, the line between the brows that were drawn together above the forceful line of his nose, the austerity of his cheekbones and the dark, almost sooty lashes that shielded his eyes. There was something guarded about the way he held himself, she thought. He had the closed-in look of a man who had been on his own a long time, a steely reserve that managed to repel and intrigue her at the same time.

Lizzy's gaze fell to the beautifully tailored suit, the designer shirt and tie, the immaculately clean nails. It was impossible to imagine him dirty and sweaty, coughing in the swirling dust or wrestling a scrubber bull to the ground. He belonged in the hard-edged world of a city skyscraper, all electronic efficiency and stream-lined technology. Sure, he could set up an office in the homestead, but what would be the point?

'Are you really thinking about going to live at Barra Creek?' she asked him, unable to conceal the disbelief in her voice.

'Yes.'

'But...*why*?'

'Because it's my home.' Tye looked up from the table, and as always Lizzy was startled by the lightness of his eyes against those dark lashes. It was like receiving a tiny electric shock every time.

'For the last twenty years I've been able to go anywhere in the world,' he went on, 'except the one place I wanted to be—Barra. It's where I was born, where I grew up. The land there is part of me.'

His eyes dropped back to his glass, and without them drilling into her Lizzy could breathe again. 'I've lived in New York,' he said. 'I've been to all those cities you mentioned and I feel about them the way you feel about the outback. They're OK for a while, but they're not where I want to be. They're all the same. I can stand in any GCS office around the world and look out and all I see is concrete and cars. There's not enough sky in a city. I sit in my office and I think about what it would be like to be back at Barra, riding through the ranges, mustering the long paddocks, swimming in the creek...'

Tye pushed the glass abruptly to one side and sat back, and the look he sent Lizzy was half-shame-faced, half-defiant, as if he were afraid that he had given too much away.

Nonplussed, she stared back at him. There had been a note in his voice when he talked about Barra that she had never heard before. Who would have thought that Tye Gibson could feel like that? Tye, the quintessential capitalist, with his hard eyes and his ruthless mouth. If asked, Lizzy would have said without hesitation that all he cared about was making money, but now it seemed that she would have been wrong.

'Why have you waited until now?' she asked, puzzled. 'You could have bought a hundred properties.'

'I didn't want another property,' said Tye flatly. 'I only wanted Barra.'

'But if you feel that strongly about it, why did you leave?'

His face closed. 'I had to go—and once I had my father wouldn't let me come home.' The grey eyes were bitter as he met Lizzy's shocked gaze. 'Yes, good old Frank Gibson who was said to be so broken-hearted by my departure! People around Mathison respected him, didn't they? They thought he was a fine, upstanding man, firm but fair.' He mimicked the way people might have talked about his father. 'Not the easiest of men, perhaps, but you knew where you were with him. Isn't that right?'

Lizzy shifted uncomfortably in her seat. 'More or less.'

Tye nodded grimly. 'They only ever saw one side of him. My father was an obsessive. He made my mother's life a misery, and when she left he took out his feelings at what he thought of as her betrayal on me. I was only seven and he was determined to bring me up so that he could control me the way he hadn't been able to control her. He refused to let her have any contact with me at all, and instead he dictated what I ate, what I wore, what I did every minute of the day.'

Lizzy had been listening in appalled disbelief, moved more by what he hadn't said than by what he had. That casual reference to his mother leaving, abandoning a small boy to a brutally authoritarian father... Had any of those who had been so quick to pass judgement on

Tye as a troublemaker ever stopped to wonder what his childhood had been like, isolated and unhappy, with no one to comfort or console him or to kiss things better?

Belatedly realising that her nails were digging into her palms, Lizzy forced herself to unclench her fists. She wished she could tell him how sorry she felt for the little boy he had been, but she sensed that Tye was not the kind of man who would welcome sympathy.

'How did you cope?' she asked instead

'I rebelled.' Tye's mouth twisted at the memory of growing up. 'I'd go out looking for trouble, and if I didn't find it, I would make it. Dad's response was to try and restrict me even further, and that only made me worse. It was inevitable that it would all end badly.'

'What happened?' asked Lizzy hesitantly.

Tye shrugged. 'We had a blazing row. Now I can't even remember how it started, but it turned nasty very quickly, and I told him I'd had enough and that I wanted to go away for a while. Dad refused to even consider the idea. He told me he had "plans" for me.'

'What kind of plans?'

'The kind that would enable him to keep me and Barra right under his control. He wanted me to settle down, get married to a nice, suitable girl and have a son who would inherit Barra.'

Lizzy's mind boggled as she tried to imagine the scene. 'What did you say?'

'I laughed in his face,' said Tye with grim satisfaction. 'I was only twenty, for God's sake, and I told him that even if I'd been ten years older, having had him as an example of husband and father, there was no way I was ever getting married or having children!'

'He can't have liked that very much.'

Tye looked at her. 'That's one way of putting it,' he

agreed somewhat sardonically. 'I'd never seen him as angry as he was that day. He knew it was crunch time. For him, giving in or compromising would have been surrendering his control, and he wasn't prepared to do that. He didn't think he would have to, either. He knew how I felt about Barra, and he played what he thought was his trump card. He told me that if I left I would never be able to come back. I could go, but as far as he was concerned, I would no longer be his son, and if I ever set foot on Barra again he would meet me with a shotgun and shoot me like a roo.'

What did you say to someone whose father had said something like that? Lizzy bit her lip and looked down at her hands. 'I'm sorry,' she muttered.

Tye lifted his shoulders in a tiny shrug, as if acknowledging the inadequacy of her response. 'In some ways my father's ultimatum was a good thing. If things had been different I would have stayed at Barra all my life and never seen or done anything else. As it was, I chose freedom and independence, but Barra was the price I paid. I left the next day.'

What had it been like for him? Lizzy wondered. Twenty wasn't that old to be disowned by a father and forced to make your own way in the world far away from the place you loved. No wonder he had learnt to be guarded.

'And you never went back?'

Tye shook his head. 'Last week, when I came to your sister's wedding, was the first time I'd been to Barra Creek for almost twenty years.'

He glanced at Lizzy, and the bleakness in his grey eyes gave her a glimpse of what those years had been like. 'I feel as if I've spent all that time in exile,' he said. 'I'm not looking for sympathy. I've done well in those years. I've built up a successful company and made all the money I need. My only ambition now is to go home.'

Lizzy couldn't imagine not being able to go home whenever she wanted. She might grumble about her parents' life in the outback, but she took it for granted that they would always be there when she needed them. On more than one occasion, when things had got too much, she had found herself heading back to the rambling, slightly shabby homestead where she had grown up, and been comforted by the familiar routines of family life.

'At least you know you're going to achieve your ambition,' she said, trying to lighten the mood. 'That's more than I can say! Barra is yours now, and you can go back whenever you want.'

'Yes,' Tye agreed after a moment, but there was a flintiness in his expression that Lizzy didn't understand.

Wondering what had caused the newly grim set to his mouth, she cast around for something to say to break the lengthening silence. 'Aren't you afraid of being lonely?' she asked at last.

'Lonely?' Tye sounded as if he didn't know what the word meant.

'Barra is a big place,' she pointed out. 'One man could feel a bit lost in a million acres.'

'There are still stockmen there,' he pointed out, 'and there'll be the staff from my Sydney apartment. I've sent up a team to get the homestead ready.'

Lizzy tried and failed to picture Tye sitting around at smoko between a tough ringer and a Sydney chef. 'Right,' she said, keeping her inevitable conclusions to herself.

'And then,' said Tye, leaning forward to look into her face, 'there'll be you.'

Lizzy found her nervously wandering gaze trapped by his eyes. They held an expression that she couldn't decipher, but they weren't cold. They weren't cold at all. Lizzy felt like the wallabies you saw on the road at night, frozen in the headlights. Like them, she could only stare helplessly back at him and long for the strength to look away, make a light comment to break the atmosphere, while her pulse boomed in her ears and a strange quivery feeling grew inside her.

'I hope,' Tye added softly, and then, unfairly, he smiled.

It was the smile Lizzy remembered so vividly from Ellie's wedding; the smile that banished the grimness from his face; the smile he had smiled as he left her at the woolshed door, her lips still burning from his kiss and her senses afire. Desperately, she tried to resist its charm, breaking it down into component parts as if analysing it would destroy its magic.

So it was a smile that illuminated his eyes and warmed the severe angles of his face? That happened when anyone smiled. Anyone's mouth would curve, and the creases in their cheek on either side would deepen. That was what a smile was. OK, so Tye's teeth looked particularly strong and white in his dark face, but what was there in that to make the air around them evaporate as her heart jerked and her insides snarled themselves into a knot?

Lizzy managed to take a breath. There, it wasn't that difficult, after all, was it?

'Right,' she said weakly again.

CHAPTER FOUR

A LIMOUSINE was waiting for them outside the hotel entrance, its engine idling. As Tye and Lizzy came out the chauffeur leapt into action and opened the door. Feeling very conspicuous, Lizzy got in. She had never been to anything like the restaurant where they eventually pulled up, although she had read about it in the gourmet magazines that she liked to flick through sometimes.

She recognised several celebrities as they followed the waiter to their table, and it was an odd sensation to realise that heads were turning to look at them as they passed, rather than the other way round. Tye's reluctance to be interviewed meant that his photo hardly ever appeared in the papers, and probably few people there knew who he was, but, as Lizzy knew only too well, he was the kind of man who got noticed anyway.

He had a quality of magnetism, an air of raw, coiled power held in check that drew the eye. He walked through the restaurant the way a panther might prowl through the jungle, lean and lithe and utterly self-contained.

At any other time Lizzy would have revelled in the attention. With anyone else she would have been thrilled by the sheer glamour of the evening. The champagne, the limousine, the fabulous food and immaculate service, the whispered speculation of the other diners, an attractive man sitting across the table... Lizzy had dreamed about an evening like this.

It wasn't fair, she thought. She should have been having the time of her life, but all she could think about was Tye and the way he had smiled. It had left her with a buzzy feeling under her skin, and an intense awareness of her surroundings that sharpened her senses and made her excruciatingly conscious of tiny details that she had never noticed before. The feel of the zip, cool and metallic against her spine. The crisp sound as she unfolded the linen napkin. The smell of coriander drifting from a nearby table.

And Tye, reading the menu, his hands holding the card, his face dark and intent.

Lizzy tried to concentrate on her own menu, but her eyes kept sliding back to him. What was it about him that made him so compelling? He didn't do anything to attract attention. Quite the reverse. He was a man who gave nothing away.

She wondered what the other diners made of the guarded face with its harsh features, and the mouth that could smile so devastatingly set once more in the grim line that seemed more natural to it.

If she had been sitting on the other side of the restaurant, she would probably have put him down as a ruthless businessman. She wouldn't have been able to guess at the bleak childhood or the depth of his feelings for the land he had lost for so long. She would have written him off as humourless and arrogant without being able to see the complexity that lay beneath the hard surface. She wouldn't have known how swiftly and unexpectedly his smile could transform him into someone quite different.

Someone warmer, more likeable. Someone disturbingly attractive.

'Are you ready to order?'

Tye's voice broke into her thoughts and Lizzy started and flushed a bright red. 'Er...not yet,' she muttered, burying her face in the menu. The letters danced before her eyes, forming themselves into the shape of his dark face with its cool, ironic expression and the faint lift of his brows as he caught her gazing soulfully at him.

She must get a grip! Lizzy's eyes almost crossed in the effort to focus on the stylish script, and her cheeks burned at the thought of how she must have looked. To anyone watching it would look as if she and Tye were on a date, but she knew better, didn't she?

For a brief moment Lizzy allowed herself to wonder what it would be like if this *were* a date, if she was there because Tye found her attractive and wanted her near, before she quashed the image firmly. It was completely unconvincing for a start. There was no way an ordinary girl like her would ever blend with his décor.

He wasn't interested in her blue eyes. He just wanted to know how suitable she was for this mysterious job of his. The setting might be romantic, Lizzy reminded herself, but this was still an interview, and she had better not forget it.

But it was all too easy to forget when outside the window the harbour lights shimmered on the dark water and Tye was sitting opposite her, turning his glass absently between his fingers. For Lizzy, the evening had taken on an air of unreality. Perhaps it was the champagne she had drunk before she arrived, but she felt curiously detached from everything that was going on around her. The other diners had receded into a blur at the edge of her vision, no more than a faint murmur in the background.

Plates appeared and disappeared in front of her, and the food looked sublime, but later Lizzy would have no memory of what she had eaten or, indeed, of what had been said. Tye talked, and she supposed that she must have answered, but afterwards she would have no recollection of their conversation.

It was as if there were two Lizzys at the table: one who could eat and drink and speak, and another who was aware only of the pulse beating in Tye's throat, of the line of his jaw, of the way his fingers curled around the stem of his glass. There was a slow, steady thumping deep inside her that grew more and more insistent, until even the first Lizzy, the bright, chatty Lizzy, who smiled and laughed and claimed that the food was delicious, began to falter. She would start to say something, only to find herself sticking in the middle of a sentence as her eyes became riveted on his mouth or his hands, and the remorseless thump would boom in her ears and she would lose her drift, swamped by the memory of his touch.

It was a relief when Tye signalled for the bill. Outside, Lizzy took a deep breath of fresh air. She had drunk too much wine, that was all that was the matter with her. She shook her head as if to clear it, and Tye, tucking his credit card back inside his jacket, glanced at her.

'Are you all right?'

'Yes…yes…I'm fine.' The fresh air didn't seem to be making that much difference. Lizzy's eyes skittered frantically around, from the buildings opposite to the lamp posts, to the great, gleaming limousine that waited with its engine purring patiently, to anywhere except Tye's face. 'I was just thinking what a beautiful night it is,' she said desperately in an attempt to explain her strange behaviour.

Tye looked up at the overcast sky.

'It's not raining,' she explained defiantly.

'True.' There was a thread of amusement in his voice. 'Shall we walk for a bit?'

Lizzy swallowed. 'OK.'

As he turned, Tye's eyes were caught by her frivolous shoes. He frowned down at the jaunty feathers and narrow heels. 'Can you walk in those? Perhaps we'd better go in the car after all.'

'No,' said Lizzy quickly. Too quickly. 'They're fine. I'd like to walk.'

Getting in the car would mean that the evening was almost over. Lizzy watched Tye as he went over to the limousine and told the chauffeur to wait, and a feeling like a cold stone settled in her stomach.

Oh, Lizzy! she sighed to herself. Don't be a fool!

She should have said that she wanted to go straight back to the hotel. She should have wished Tye a cool goodnight and shut herself in her room and remembered all the reasons why she didn't like him. She should have told him that she had only come to hear about the job, and, since he obviously wasn't going to tell her anything, she might as well go home at once.

And what had she done instead? She had jumped at the chance of walking alone through the dark with him, where there would be nothing and nobody to remind her of hard reality, and only her own will to stop her succumbing to the desire uncoiling uncontrollably inside her.

This is an interview. An interview. An *interview*, Lizzy chanted to herself as she fell into step beside Tye. Her hands twitched with the longing to reach out, to stop him, to make him turn towards her so that she could slide them up his arms to his shoulders and pull his head down to hers. Terrified that they would stretch out of their own accord, Lizzy hugged her arms together in front of her and stared fixedly ahead.

Her body pounded. The deep, remorseless thump had spread outwards until it beat through her, throbbing along her veins and pulsing beneath her skin, quivering at the tips of her fingers, shivering down to the very ends of her hair. It felt as if she were running a fever.

Lizzy clutched at the possibility. Perhaps I am. Perhaps I'm ill.

But she didn't stop and ask to be taken back to the hotel.

They walked in silence. Absorbed in his own thoughts, Tye had his hands thrust into his trouser pockets, his shoulders hunched slightly forward. Lizzy was beginning to wonder whether he had forgotten that she was there when he stopped and looked down at her.

'How are the feet?'

'Feet?' said Lizzy blankly.

'Your shoes don't look too comfortable.'

She looked down. By rights she should have been limping and wincing at her pinched toes, but somehow tonight her feet seemed the least of her problems. 'No, they're fine.'

A silence fell. They had been walking along the harbour edge, and as if by unspoken agreement they turned to lean on the wall and look at the reflections of the lights rocking gently in the oily sheen that lay in patches on the water.

The famous bridge soared above them, and further along Lizzy could see the distinctive outline of the opera house, floodlit against the dark sky. Here she was in the heart of one of the most beautiful, exciting cities in the world, she thought with something like despair, and all she could think about was the man beside her!

It wasn't even as if they were alone. The traffic rumbled across the bridge; a ferry steamed across the harbour. A group of Japanese tourists went past them, exclaiming excitedly, and somewhere in the distance a siren wailed. But Lizzy and Tye seemed trapped in a soundless bubble, cut off from the rest of the world by an invisible barrier.

The silence lengthened unnervingly. They glanced at each other and then away. Lizzy pressed her palms against the rough stones, as if anchoring herself to reality, but her gaze kept slithering sideways to rest hungrily on the hard, exciting line of his cheek, on the edge of his mouth.

He wasn't handsome, Lizzy thought with a kind of desperation. She didn't even like him very much. He was cold and hard and bitterly self-contained. She might have more sympathy for him since she had learnt more of his story, but that didn't make him a warm, wonderful human being. Tye was never going to be kind, or considerate. He wasn't even fun.

So why did he make her feel like this? Restless and giddy and racked with a terrible, treacherous longing at the mere thought of touching him.

Without warning, Tye turned his head, and Lizzy's heart gave a great jerk as she found herself trapped by his eyes.

'You're very quiet,' he said. 'What are you thinking about?'

About the feel of your skin, she wanted to say. About the touch of your hands. About the hardness of your body and what it would be like to put my arms around you and press my lips to that pulse in the side of your neck.

About what it would be like to kiss you. Not a peck

on the cheek, not a brief brush of the lips, but a real kiss.

'Oh…nothing,' she said instead, her voice high and unsteady. 'I'm only quiet because I didn't want to interrupt you. I thought *you* were thinking.'

'I was,' said Tye.

'What about?'

'About you.'

The air leaked out of Lizzy's lungs as he straightened, and without thinking she straightened as well, until they stood facing each other, still not touching but bound together by an invisible current that crackled between them.

Lizzy's pulse was thundering in her ears. 'About whether you can trust me?' she asked with difficulty, her mouth so dry that she could hardly get the words out.

'Among other things.' Tye looked down into her face. Her eyes were wide and dark, and he reached out to let a careless finger drift tantalisingly down her cheek to the corner of her mouth. 'I think I could,' he said softly.

Lizzy stared dumbly back at him, her skin burning from that casual caress and her heart slamming against her ribs.

'Couldn't I?' said Tye.

She nodded.

'Good,' he said. His voice deepened as the light eyes dropped to her mouth. 'Do you want to know what else I was thinking about?'

'What?' she whispered, barely aware of what she was saying, conscious only of the desire drumming inside her.

In response, Tye cupped her face gently between his palms. 'About this,' he said, smiling, and he bent his head very slowly towards hers.

Swamped by a wave of anticipation and giddy relief, Lizzy closed her eyes, and the next moment his mouth came down on hers and the world spun dazzlingly around her. Incapable of resisting, even if she had wanted to, she leant into him, her lips opening responsively beneath his and her arms sliding under his jacket to pull him closer. She was beyond being sensible, beyond thinking about anything except the glorious fact that she was kissing him the way, deep down, she had been thinking about kissing him all evening.

And Tye was kissing her, a real kiss, the kiss she had been dreaming about as she leant beside him on the wall, but better. This kiss was electrifying, intoxicating, and her response was so intense that Lizzy was almost frightened. There was no ground beneath her feet, no bridge, no opera house. The harbour had gone, dissolving around her as she was swept into a vortex of whirling excitement where there was nothing but Tye's mouth and his hands, sliding down her throat, gathering her closer to him, deepening the kiss.

Lizzy was gasping and breathless when his lips left hers to drift seductively along her jaw. She arched her throat with a shudder of pleasure as she felt Tye kiss the lobe of her ear.

'Is…is this part of the interview?' she murmured, smiling shakily, certain that she would feel him smile back against her skin and deny it, that he would kiss her again and convince her that he wanted her the way she so wanted him.

But Tye didn't smile. He stilled, his lips against her temple, and the sudden tautness of his body sent a trickle of apprehension down Lizzy's spine.

She pulled herself away so that she could look into his face. '*Is* it?'

'In a way,' he admitted.

Lizzy's arms fell, and she backed away from him until she came up against the wall and could brace herself against the great, boiling wave of humiliation that crashed over her. What had he been thinking as he kissed her? Had there been a part of his mind coolly calculating her response, amused by her eagerness, perhaps assessing with clinical detachment just how far she would go?

Lizzy felt sick. How could she have forgotten what Tye was like? Had she really thought that he would lose control of the situation that easily? He was a man who always knew exactly what he was doing, and why.

'I think you'd better tell me exactly what it is you want me for,' she said in a frozen voice.

'I need a wife.'

There was a long, long silence.

'A what?' said Lizzy at last.

'You heard.'

She moistened her lips. 'You're asking me to marry you?' Her voice was husky with disbelief, and Tye smiled faintly but without much humour.

'I don't seem to be going about it very well, but I guess that's just what I am doing.'

Lizzy pressed her hands to her temples to try and steady her reeling head. She felt utterly disorientated, still drenched with the intoxication of his kiss, that lingered in spite of the bitter disgust that had hit her like a slap in the face, and now struggling to accept Tye's incredible announcement.

'But you...you don't want to get married,' she stammered. Hadn't he said that? Hadn't he stood at Ellie's wedding and sneered at the very idea? Or had that happened in some parallel universe where everything made sense and not the one she found herself in now?

'I do now,' said Tye. 'I have to get married before I'm forty. That's only two months away.'

Lizzy's hands fell from her head, but her mind still spun crazily. 'You're…joking…' she managed, still stuttering incredulously.

Tye shook his head, and his mouth twisted into a bitter smile. 'I wish I was.'

He looked down at his hands, as if wondering what to do with them, thrusting them into pockets as he turned to face the harbour.

'My father left me Barra Creek, but on one condition,' he said flatly. 'I can have Barra, but only if I get married, and only if my wife is an Australian, born and bred in the outback.'

Lizzy stared at him. 'But surely that's not legal!' she protested.

'Do you think I haven't had my entire legal department combing the will for loopholes?' Tye almost snarled. 'It's legal all right. If I want Barra Creek, I have to find myself a wife.'

'And that's the job? Marrying you?'

'Yes.'

A glorious surge of anger propelled Lizzy upright from where she had collapsed, shaken, against the wall. It came out of nowhere, exploding in a burst of adrenalin the like of which Lizzy had never experienced before. Invigorated, even exhilarated, she faced Tye with blazing eyes.

'So tonight—the champagne, the limousine, the dinner—that's what it was all about?' Her voice shook, but this time with fury rather than distress. 'You needed someone to marry, and you thought I'd do? Poor old Lizzy Walker, well into her thirties and still single! She must be desperate! Is that what you thought?'

'No,' said Tye, but she hardly heard him.

'I bet you thought it would be easy. All you had to do was lay on the luxury to impress me. It wouldn't take much to bowl over a country girl like me, would it? A bit of French champagne and a chauffeur, and I'd jump at the idea of marrying you!'

'It wasn't like that,' Tye began, his voice tightening, but Lizzy was too angry to listen.

'And that kiss just now?' she demanded furiously. 'What was *that* about? Extra insurance in case all that money dangled in front of my nose hadn't quite done trick? Or did you think that I was so desperate I'd fall into the arms of the first man who showed me a little attention? A cheap date like me: you should have skipped the champagne and gone straight for a spot of lovemaking! Is that what you were thinking?'

'No!' Tye shouted back at her, and a couple who were passing looked curiously at them as they faced each other angrily. A muscle pounded in his cheek, and he made a visible effort to control himself.

'No,' he said again, more quietly this time. 'That wasn't what I was thinking when I kissed you.'

'What *were* you thinking, then?' Lizzy had seen the looks passers-by were giving them, and she lowered her voice too, but her face was still tense and white.

'I wasn't thinking at all,' said Tye. 'That was the trouble.'

They stared at each other, and the jangling antagonism leaked out of the air to be replaced by the memory of that kiss. It shimmered between them, disturbing, tantalising, and Lizzy's fury evaporated as quickly as it had erupted, leaving her empty and confused and perilously close to tears. Tye's kiss might have been calculating, but she had so nearly fallen for it.

'I don't believe this!' she muttered, turning her face away.

Tye sighed and raked his fingers through his hair. 'Look, I'm sorry. I've gone about this all the wrong way. Will you just let me explain?'

'I don't think I want to hear it.'

'You said I could trust you.' He hesitated. 'Please, Lizzy?'

Tye Gibson begging. Now there was a turn-up for the books, thought Lizzy bitterly. 'Please' wasn't a word that he would use very often.

Her body was still trembling with reaction, and humiliating tears prickled her eyes. She didn't want to listen to Tye explaining why he had made a fool out of her, but that wonderful, invigorating anger had fizzled away, and she made the mistake of looking at Tye. He was watching her with a serious expression, and something in his eyes made her nod her head.

'All right,' she said dully.

Tye let out a breath. 'I don't know about you, but I could use a drink,' he said. 'Let's go and sit down.'

He took her arm and led back to a café they had passed earlier. It felt like a lifetime ago, thought Lizzy, letting him sit her at a table in a quiet corner. Too weary and confused to protest, she waited until he came back and put a glass in her hand.

'Drink that,' he said. Gulping obediently, Lizzy choked and spluttered as the fiery liquid burned down her throat. Her eyes watered, but it had steadied her. She set the glass on the table, no longer feeling as if she were teetering on the edge of hysteria.

'Better?'

'Yes.' She nodded, even managing a shaky smile.

Tye sat down next to her and swirled the brandy

around his own glass, obviously choosing his words carefully.

'Contrary to popular belief, I didn't just abandon my father—or Barra,' he said. 'From time to time I would ring him, but he always hung up at the sound of my voice, and after a while I admit that I gave up. I'd moved to the States and was preoccupied with business, but a few years ago I tried again.

'I knew that Dad was getting older and that he would need help running Barra, so I wrote to him, suggesting that I came back and took on some of the responsibility. He didn't answer, but I got a letter back from his lawyer, who said that my father had already made his position clear and was not prepared to discuss the matter further. In other words, I could only go home if I agreed to get married. And *I* wasn't prepared to do *that*.'

Tye glanced at Lizzy. She was still looking shocked, but at least she was listening. 'I know it sounds callous, but at that point I really did give up. I told myself that I was just going to have to wait until he died before I could go home. Barra was the only thing Dad and I had in common, and I was sure that he wouldn't leave it to anyone other than his son.'

He laughed mirthlessly. 'I should have known better! Dad had his plan, and he'd waited a long time to get his own way. He wanted me married, and Barra passed on to a new generation of Gibsons, so he inserted that clause into his will. I could have Barra, but only if I did what he had wanted me to do all along.

'He was very specific,' he added bitterly. 'I had to get married before I was forty, and I couldn't choose anyone I wanted. My mother was English and a city girl, and that marriage was a disaster. There was no way Dad was letting anyone like her back on Barra. That's why he

insisted on me marrying an outback girl, the kind of
woman he thought was suitable to bring up Gibson children. The lawyers have to be satisfied that my wife ful-
fils his conditions before Barra legally becomes mine.'

'I can't believe a father would do anything like that,'
said Lizzy helplessly.

'I can,' said Tye. 'His will was Dad's last chance to
get his own way. He'd refused to let me back to Barra
for twenty years, but that hadn't worked. Barra was the
ace up his sleeve. He knew how much it meant to me,
and that it was the one thing that would get me to do
what he wanted.'

He smiled grimly. 'I'll bet Dad enjoyed putting that
clause in the will, knowing I'd be counting on the fact
that Barra would be mine in the end. He must have
thought he'd hit on the perfect way to control me, even
if he wasn't going to have the satisfaction of seeing me
knuckle under!'

'What happens if you don't get married?' she asked,
cradling her glass between her hands as if for comfort.

'Barra goes to a distant relative—the son of one of
Dad's cousins. Dad would have chosen him because his
surname is Gibson, although he would have been betting
on the fact that I wouldn't let it come to that. I don't
know anything about this Paul Gibson, other than the
fact that he lives in Brisbane and has never been near
Barra in his life.' Bitterness slipped back into Tye's
voice. 'Barra wouldn't mean anything to him.'

'Well…couldn't you get married and then divorced?'

'I thought of that, but Dad had it all covered. He
wasn't going to have the future of Barra threatened by
any divorce. He wanted me settled, with a sensible wife
and children, the way he'd planned it all along. So the

will specifies that the day I get divorced, the property reverts to Paul Gibson.'

He took a mouthful of brandy as if he needed it. 'You can't say my father didn't think of everything,' he said.

Lizzy was beginning to understand his bitterness. 'So you have a straight choice? Marry, or lose Barra.'

'That's it.' Tye pushed his glass aside. 'When his lawyer told me about the condition in the will, I was so angry I couldn't think straight. I'd spent my whole life trying to get away from my father's control, and now if I wanted Barra I'd have to give in. I'd sworn I would never let anyone else run my life for me. I'd have to give up my independence, marry the kind of girl he'd wanted me to marry all along... I decided I couldn't do it. It would be like letting him control the rest of my life. And then I went back to sort out his things.'

Tye stopped, remembering how he had felt that day. 'It was the first time I'd been to Barra in twenty years. It was only when I went back that I realised quite how much I'd missed it. It was...' He trailed off, frowning down at his hands. 'I can't tell you what it was like,' he admitted eventually. 'Nothing had changed. Part of me still wants to say to hell with my father, but...'

He looked into Lizzy's eyes, his own very clear and direct. 'I want to go back,' he said simply. 'And to go back I have to have a wife.'

Lizzy tore her gaze away and stared fixedly down at the glass she was turning between her hands on the table. 'So that's why you came to Ellie's wedding,' she said dully.

'Yes,' he acknowledged. 'I'd only just made my decision and I was still feeling bitter about it. When your father invited me, I thought I might as well go along. I'd have to get to know people eventually, and it seemed as good an opportunity as any to start. But I soon realised it wasn't going to be that easy to find a wife. There were plenty of people there who remembered me from my wild days, and they made it very clear they didn't want anything to do with me.'

Lizzy remembered him in the woolshed, coolly observing the crowd. He had been assessing them all, she realised indignantly, examining the women like so many cows.

'So what made you pick on me as a suitable wife?' she asked, a brittle edge to her voice.

'You were different.' Tye turned slightly in his seat to look at her. 'You were the only person there prepared to talk to me, for a start. And you looked different,' he said slowly, as if picturing her as she had been that day, with her bright face and the blue dress and the ridiculous shoes. 'You had style. The more I found out about you, the better you seemed. You might be a city girl now, but you were born and bred in the outback, and everyone agreed what a nice girl you were. My father's executors couldn't possibly object to you.'

'Oh, well, that's all right, then,' said Lizzy sarcastically, ruffled by the realisation of how carefully he had been looking her over.

'When you caught that bouquet…' He smiled slightly. 'Well, I'm not a great believer in omens, but I did begin to wonder if somebody was trying to tell me something! I knew then that you were single, which was the main thing, and you were attractive.'

Tye glanced at Lizzy's hostile face. 'I'm not pretending I fell madly in love with you, Lizzy. I've never wanted to get married, but I knew that I had to find someone, and when I looked around that woolshed I realised that I'd as soon marry you as anyone else.'

'Gee, thanks!'

'My next step was to find a way to see you again,' he went on, ignoring her sarcastic interjection. 'It was a stroke of luck when you told me that you were in PR and setting up on your own. I know what the market is like at the moment, and knew there was a good chance that you'd be looking for work.'

'You mean there was a good chance of me falling for that line about a job,' said Lizzy bitterly. 'That must have given you a laugh, letting me think that I could salvage my career, when all the time—'

She broke off as everything began to fall into place. 'And that kiss!' she remembered furiously. 'There was no need for me to make an exhibition of myself in front of all those people, was there?'

'On the contrary. It told me a lot about you.' To Lizzy's chagrin, a gleam of humour lit Tye's eyes. 'If you'd been the kind of girl who was swayed by what other people thought, there would have been no point in getting to know you any better.'

He paused. 'But you aren't that kind of girl, are you, Lizzy?' he said.

'I was desperate for a job,' said Lizzy defensively. 'I would never have kissed you otherwise.'

'And this evening?' he asked.

The blue eyes fell, and colour washed into her face as she remembered how she had melted into his arms. 'You should have told me,' she muttered. 'I thought I was being interviewed all evening.'

That wasn't quite true, and she knew it. She hadn't been thinking about a job when she walked beside him in the dark, when she kissed him by the water.

'I couldn't tell you straight out,' said Tye. 'I knew that you'd never have agreed if I'd told you that I was looking for a wife and not a PR consultant. I wanted you to know what Barra meant to me. I wanted to try and make you understand why I had to get married, and I had to be sure that you wouldn't run straight off to the papers with the story.

'That's why I said I had to trust you,' he said, his eyes on Lizzy's face. 'That's why I'm trusting you now.'

CHAPTER FIVE

'YOU said you wanted to be married, Lizzy,' Tye reminded her when she only looked away.

'Not like this!'

'The end result is the same. This way we could both achieve our ambitions. I could have Barra and you could have marriage, a family even, if that's what you want.'

A little colour crept into Lizzy's cheeks at the idea of having children with Tye. It was alarmingly intimate, and embarrassment at her own embarrassment sharpened her voice. 'You can't treat being a wife as if it's some kind of job! What were you proposing to do, offer me a salary?'

'You wouldn't need a salary,' said Tye, ignoring her scorn and answering her quite seriously. 'As my wife, you would be a very wealthy woman. You'd be able to do whatever you wanted.'

'Except divorce you,' she pointed out tartly.

He shrugged. 'I wouldn't interfere with you. You could be as independent as you wanted as long as you were legally married to me. You wouldn't even need to sleep with me if you didn't want to,' he said with a sideways glance at Lizzy's hot face.

'You could have a lover, buy yourself an apartment in New York, live exactly the way you want to live. All you'd have to do is spend enough time with me at Barra to convince my father's executors that our marriage was genuine. That wouldn't be too hard, would it?'

'That's not what marriage is about,' protested Lizzy,

shuddering at the mere idea of such a cold-hearted arrangement. 'It's not about money or independence. It's about commitment. It's about sharing.' She looked down at her hands in her lap. 'It's about love.'

'Oh, *love*...' Tye's voice was laced with contempt. 'I might have known you'd bring that up!'

'It's important,' said Lizzy stubbornly.

'It's an illusion,' he retorted. 'I'm not going to insult your intelligence by pretending that I'm in love with you, Lizzy, but I think we could still have a lot going for us. There are lots of things about you that I like. I like the way you look. I like the way you talk.' He paused, and a smile crept into his voice. 'I like the way you kiss.'

Lizzy steeled herself against the charm. She wasn't going to fall for that smile again! 'You like the way marrying me would net you a million-acre cattle station!' she said with a tart look.

'That too,' Tye agreed equably. 'I think it would be enough to make a marriage work.'

'Assuming that there are enough things that *I* like about *you*!' she pointed out crossly.

'Aren't there?'

'Right at this moment, I can't think of *any*!'

'You like kissing me,' he said unfairly. 'And don't try to deny it,' he added, as Lizzy opened her mouth.

She shut it again with something of a snap and eyed Tye with hostility. 'It's not enough,' she said after a moment.

Tye drew in a sharp breath of frustration. 'What exactly is it that you want?' he asked, struggling to contain his impatience.

What did she want? Lizzy laid her hands on the table and studied them. 'I want someone to love,' she said slowly. 'Not someone I'm fond of, or someone I desire, but someone I *need*. Someone who'll always be there, to hold me and keep me safe and make me laugh when I'm down. Someone to be the other half of me.' She raised her eyes to meet Tye's steadily. 'I want someone who'll feel exactly the same about me,' she told him.

There was a tiny silence, then Tye looked away almost irritably. 'That's just a romantic dream,' he said. 'Life isn't like that.'

Lizzy thought of Gray and Clare, of her sister just starting her married life with Jack. 'It can be.'

'How often?' demanded Tye. 'How long are you going to hold out for this mythical someone, Lizzy? Five years? Ten? You're—what? Thirty-four?'

'Thirty-three,' she put in quickly.

'OK, thirty-three. Time's still running out. You're living in a dream world, Lizzy. There's no such thing as a perfect relationship, and one day you're going to wake up and realise that you've wasted your life waiting for something that doesn't exist. I may not be your ideal man, but at least I'm real,' he said.

'You turn your nose up at money,' he went on, 'but think about what a difference it could make. No more worrying about your mortgage or paying off your credit cards. You can go shopping in Paris, pop up to Hong Kong for the weekend, buy as many shoes as you want.

'I can offer you financial security,' said Tye, at his most persuasive, 'and I can give you emotional security too, if that's what you want. I've never wanted to be a father—not after my own experience—but we could have children. Why not? A new generation to grow up at Barra. You could be a mother, Lizzy. OK, so we wouldn't have the perfect love you've dreamed about, but we'd have a relationship based on sexual attraction

and respect. Marriages have been built on a lot less than
that. Don't dismiss the idea out of hand.'

What would it be like to be married to Tye? Lizzy let
herself imagine being his wife, learning how to read his
moods, knowing how he took his coffee. She would
know what he looked like when he woke up, the way
he slept. The way he made love.

Her mouth dried at the thought. His body would be
utterly familiar to her. She would be able to run her
hands over him, to explore his hardness, to taste his skin.
She would be able to smile when he rolled over in bed
and reached for her.

Something warm and treacherous stirred inside Lizzy.
She felt it uncoil insidiously and trickle down to clench
at the base of her spine, and she checked her wandering
thoughts with an effort.

What was she doing even *thinking* about it? She
should be thinking about Clare and the way she looked
at Gray, about the expression on Ellie's face when Jack
kissed her. *That* was what she wanted, Lizzy reminded
herself almost fiercely. It was more than someone to
wake up with every morning, and a lot more than the
financial security Tye seemed to think would be so attractive to her.

If security was all she wanted, she could have married
Stephen. At least Stephen was kind and considerate, a
good friend. They would have been happy enough together, but she had known that it wouldn't be enough
for her. She didn't need security and she didn't need
money. All she needed was love.

Lizzy shook her blonde head firmly. 'It's got to be
perfect,' she told Tye. 'I'd rather not marry at all than
settle for anything less.'

'So you won't marry me?' he said after a pause.

'No.'

'What about your financial problems?'

'I'm looking for a job, not a meal ticket,' she said coldly. 'I'm sorry if you feel you've wasted an expensive bottle of champagne on me, but you're going to have to look elsewhere for a wife. I'm not for sale.'

Her mother had been right, Lizzy thought miserably as she reached behind her for the bag she had hung on the back of her chair. Tye Gibson was trouble, and she should have had nothing to do with him. She sighed at her own naivety in thinking that he would go to so much effort because he wanted a bit of help with his public relations. She had been so thrilled in the hotel lobby when he had told her that the job was hers.

Now she was going to have to start all over again.

Wearily, she made to push back her chair, but Tye caught her wrist.

'Lizzy, wait!'

'I'm not going to change my mind!'

'You want a job? I'll give you a job.'

Lizzy pulled her wrist free. 'We've been through all this,' she said angrily.

'This time I'm talking about a real job,' he said. 'If you won't marry me yourself, you can find me someone who will.'

'That's not the kind of job I had in mind,' said Lizzy in a frosty voice. 'My skills are in public relations, not matchmaking!'

'There's no reason why you shouldn't treat it as a public relations exercise,' said Tye craftily. 'Treat me as a product that you've got to sell. Change people's perceptions of me, create a new image...do whatever you have to do to get me accepted. The way things are at the moment, I wouldn't get past the first cattle grid, let alone into a homestead to meet any unmarried daughters who might make a suitable Mrs Gibson! You could change all that. You could persuade people to buy the idea of Tye Gibson as a nice guy.' His eyes glinted disconcertingly. 'If nothing else, you could regard it as a challenge!'

'It would certainly be that!' snapped Lizzy, unaccountably ruffled by his change of tack. It wasn't that she had expected him to be heartbroken at her refusal to marry him, but here he was springing his back-up plan on her without even the decency to show a bit of regret, or any attempt to make her change her mind!

'I'd make it worth your while,' Tye went on persuasively. 'On my wedding day, you'd get the equivalent of a year's salary for something less than two months' work, plus the option of taking up a position in a GCS office of your choice. I've got PR departments around the world. You could go to Los Angeles, Singapore, Rome...wherever you wanted. And if you decided to go it alone, I'd provide a glowing reference for your work as a freelance consultant.'

He glanced again at Lizzy's face, smiling faintly at the wariness of her expression. 'I'd be a good client to have in your portfolio,' he pointed out, as if she hadn't already been well aware of the fact.

It was a very generous offer, so generous that Lizzy couldn't help being suspicious. 'What exactly would I have to do for all that?' she enquired cautiously.

'Make sure I was married before my fortieth birthday.' Tye made it sound as if it were the simplest of tasks.

'I don't quite see what I could do about it,' she said. 'I can hardly go up and start wooing girls on your behalf!'

'No, but you could save me a lot of time. You know

who's single and who isn't, who's likely to have a practical approach to marriage, who's desperate enough to consider anything. Your job would be to engineer situations where I could meet the kind of girls you think are most likely and arrange an introduction. I'd do the rest. You could think of yourself as a social secretary, if you liked, smoothing my way and making sure that I'm accepted back into the community.'

She frowned. 'Why do you need me if that's all you want?'

'Because I'm a busy man. I haven't got the time to do it all myself. My father had almost twenty years to convince his neighbours that I'm not to be trusted, and I can't change that overnight. Eventually I might be able to win people round on my own, but I need help if I'm going to do it in two months. I'm forty on the sixth of June. If I'm not married by then, I might as well not bother.'

'You must employ stacks of people at GCS who could be social secretaries,' Lizzy objected.

'Not with your contacts. You know these people, Lizzy, and they like you. I saw that at your sister's wedding. If you vouched for me, I'd be halfway there!'

Lizzy was twisting the narrow strap of her bag around her hand. 'I don't know…it just sounds so callous,' she said eventually. 'Like some kind of beauty contest. I might as well herd all the available women of a certain age into the cattle yards and let you take your pick!'

'It wouldn't be like that.' Tye kept his voice steady with an effort that showed in the muscle jumping jerkily in his jaw. 'All you would have to do is introduce me around and let it be known that I'm not as bad as everyone thinks. And then, when I've made my choice, you can help me convince her that marrying me would be a good idea.'

'What if she gets hurt?' Lizzy asked.

'Hurt?' he echoed, irritation creeping into his voice. 'How's she going to get hurt?'

'Well…' Lizzy hesitated, wondering how to put it. 'She might feel more for you than you feel for her,' she said delicately. 'It's all very well for you to say that sex and security are enough, but how is she going to feel knowing that you don't care about her other than as a way to get your hands on Barra?'

'I'd be honest with her, just the way I've been honest with you,' said Tye dismissively.

Yes, and look how far it got you! Lizzy wanted to say, but didn't dare.

He scowled at her as if he had read her mind. 'We'd sort everything out before we were married. She wouldn't be able to say afterwards that she didn't know what was involved.'

Lizzy sighed. How could she explain to a man like Tye that women didn't work like that? 'It's not that easy,' she tried. 'You can't treat marriage like one of your business deals!'

'I think you can.' Tye noticed that there was still some brandy at the bottom of his glass and drained it, banging it back down on table to emphasise his point. 'Wrap it up in all the sentiment you like, but when it comes down to it marriage is an exchange of assets. Not all women are as romantic as you. I think there will be plenty who'd be prepared to do without the hearts and flowers in exchange for a share of my bank account.'

'That's an outrageous attitude!'

'Just because you think so doesn't mean everyone else has to agree with you,' he said coolly. 'If a woman understands the circumstances and makes the decision to marry me, who are you to say that she's wrong? How happy or unhappy our marriage is won't be your problem.'

It sounded reasonable enough when he put it like that, but it still felt all wrong to Lizzy. 'I don't know...' She hesitated.

'I'm offering you a job, Lizzy,' he said. 'You said you were desperate. All you have to do is spend a couple of months being sociable. How hard can that be?'

Not too hard, it had to be said. Socialising was the breath of life to Lizzy. A few weeks introducing Tye around and doing her best to convince people like her mother that he wasn't as bad as he'd been painted wasn't much to ask in exchange for a year's salary. Not to mention that tempting offer of a job with GCS. She had always liked the idea of living in New York or London...

'I can't force someone to marry you,' she pointed out. 'Do I still get paid if there's no wedding?'

He shook his head. 'Where would be the incentive in that?' he asked with one of his sardonic looks. 'I'm a believer in payment by results. You can have a flat fee to cover your costs, but the rest has to wait until my wedding day.'

'I don't know,' said Lizzy again, torn between the thought of solving her financial and career problems in one easy move and unease at the whole idea.

The blue eyes were troubled, and indecision was writ large on her mobile face. Tye leant over and took the hands that were still fiddling with her bag in a firm grasp.

'I'm not asking you to do anything illegal or immoral,' he said persuasively. 'I'm asking you to help me, Lizzy.'

His fingers were warm and strong and dangerously reassuring. Lizzy could feel his will pulsing through the touch of his skin like a physical force. It surged up her arms, banishing her doubts, vanquishing her objections, until she found it hard to remember why she was even hesitating.

'If I had more time, I could get to know people gradually and hope that they would accept me.' Lizzy dragged her attention away from his touch, frowning with the effort of concentrating on what he was saying. 'I could find a wife by myself. But I haven't got time. My father's will says that I have to be married before I'm forty. That only gives me a matter of weeks.'

To Lizzy's relief, he let go of her hands. 'I want to go home, Lizzy,' he said simply as he sat back in his chair. 'I want to go home to Barra, and I can't do it without you. Please, think about it at least.'

Lizzy's hands felt cold and oddly empty without Tye's warm clasp, and she didn't know what to do with them any more. She laid them in her lap, but that didn't feel natural, so then she rested them on the table, and that felt even worse. In the end she clasped them round her empty glass and hoped that they didn't look as conspicuous as they felt.

Tye was waiting, his light gaze fixed on her face. Lizzy's eyes flickered towards his, and then away.

'All right,' she heard herself say. 'I'll think about it.'

She thought about it all that night, tossing and turning in her hotel bed, and she thought about it the next day on the long flight back to Perth. She thought about it as she wandered restlessly around her house, Tye's words looping endlessly in her head, until she couldn't stand thinking about it any more and picked up the phone to let him know her decision.

'Good,' said Tye when she told him that she would take the job. 'You won't regret it.'

He was all briskness once the decision had been made. 'Can you get yourself to Mathison on Tuesday? I'm coming up from Sydney then. I'll pick you up at the airport, and we'll go on to Barra together.'

When Lizzy landed at Mathison on Tuesday afternoon, an executive jet with the GCS logo emblazoned on its tail was parked on the tarmac. Dragging her suitcase behind her, Lizzy headed towards it, only to be pointed to a little plane sitting further along the runway. The airstrip at Barra was apparently too rough for a jet to land, and the six-seater was waiting to take them the last stage of the journey.

Tye was already on board, tapping into a laptop computer, but he looked up as Lizzy, having handed her suitcase to the lanky pilot, clambered through the door on the wing.

'At last,' he said, exiting the system and closing the laptop with a snap. 'Now we can go.'

And that, it seemed, was all the greeting she was going to get.

Lizzy had spent the last three days trying to put that kiss by the harbour out of her mind. She'd concentrated on not thinking about it while she packed and paid her outstanding bills, and rang friends to tell them that she would be away for a couple of months. And as she'd made last-minute arrangements for visiting students to live in her house, it had seemed to Lizzy that she was a fair way to forgetting it altogether.

Considering the fact that her lips were still tingling and her pulse still fluttering and her heart still showed an alarming tendency to loop the loop whenever her thoughts strayed too close to Tye or anything that reminded her of that extraordinary evening.

And there were too many things that did that. It was almost as if the world was conspiring to make sure that she couldn't forget. All someone had to do was mention Sydney, or marriage, or champagne, and Lizzy's careful attempts to block the whole incident from her mind would come crashing down around her, swept away by a torrent of memory. Even the sight of her own palms was enough to trigger the deluge, and she would relive every moment of his kiss, and how powerful his body had felt through the fine shirt beneath her hands.

At that point Lizzy would give herself a strict talking-to. She couldn't spend the next two months falling to pieces every time she saw her hands! Endlessly, she had repeated all the reasons why taking the 'job' Tye had offered had been a good idea, and whenever she'd wavered she'd taken out her most recent bank statement, which was usually enough to persuade her that she would never again have such an opportunity to clear her debts and kick-start her career.

By the time she'd climbed into the plane at Mathison Lizzy had managed to convince herself that it would be easy. She had spent the flight up from Perth reminding herself that for the first time in her life she was going to be paid to socialise, and that couldn't be bad, could it? She might even enjoy the next two months.

The thought of spending two months with Tye Gibson was still unsettling, but Lizzy had told herself that it would be fine. She would simply pretend that the kiss had never happened, and treat him exactly as she would any other boss. All she had to do was think of him as a particularly difficult and demanding client.

Not that *that* was going to be hard, Lizzy thought, pursing her lips as she plonked herself down in the seat across from Tye's and fastened her seatbelt. He was obviously going to treat her like any other of his unfortunate employees. Honestly, she huffed to herself, you'd think he could have brought himself to say hello, after he had begged her to help him! It clearly wasn't worth his while wasting any more charm on her now that he'd got his own way.

'What's the matter with you?' Tye asked, as the propeller on the nose of the plane started to turn, slowly gathering speed until it was no more than a blur.

'Nothing,' said Lizzy with a frosty look. 'I was just reflecting that my job is going to be a lot more difficult than I'd thought. You need to acquire a few social skills before I try and introduce you to anyone!'

Having checked his instruments, the pilot began to taxi down the runway, oblivious to the conversation behind him. Tye's brows snapped together.

'What do you mean by that?'

'Oh, don't worry! I realise you won't have come across the concept before, but we can start you off on something simple like…ooh, "Hello", say, or "How are you?"!'

His countenance relaxed a bit. 'I can see how *you* are,' he said. 'Very cross!'

'Who me?' Lizzy put her hand to her throat in mock amazement. 'What have I got to be cross about? I've just spent three crazy days closing down my house, not to mention the rest of my life in Perth, at a weekend's notice, and I'm committed to spending the next two months with a man who can't even be bothered to say g'day!'

Tye rolled his eyes. 'It's just small talk,' he said. 'It

doesn't mean anything. Nobody ever really wants to know how you are, do they?'

'You've got to start somewhere,' said Lizzy crisply. 'You can't just go up to a woman, dangle your money bags in front of her nose and then ask if she feels like spending the rest of her life with you in loveless marriage! I know you think your bank balance is going to do all the talking, but I don't see you getting very far if you can't even manage to say "Nice to meet you"!'

'I'll do it when I have to and not before.' Tye's mouth turned down at the corners. 'I hate those kind of social occasions,' he admitted, loosening his tie as if he felt constricted already. 'Standing around making polite conversation with a load of people I don't know and don't want to!'

'I thought the whole point of me coming was to help you socialise!'

'It is,' he said grudgingly. 'I'm not saying I won't go; I'm just saying I'm not going to like it.'

'That's the wrong attitude for a start!' said Lizzy. 'Nobody's going to want to talk to you if you stand around looking as if you don't want to be there. You've got to relax, enjoy yourself.'

'You think I'm going to enjoy myself grovelling to all those people who've been more than happy to think the worst of me for the last twenty years, if not longer?' snarled Tye. 'Having to be pleasant to them, pretending I don't know what they think of me, trying to make them *like* me?'

His voice was raw, and it was obvious how the prospect grated on his pride. Frank Gibson had certainly picked the best way to humiliate his son, thought Lizzy with distaste.

She found herself trying to comfort Tye. 'It won't be

that bad. They're nice people. Once they get to know you, you'll be fine.'

'Easy for you to say.' He hunched a shoulder. 'I watched you at your sister's wedding.' He glanced sideways at Lizzy, as if picturing her as she had been that day, with her vivid face and her ready smile and her sympathetic blue eyes. 'You made everyone feel that they were the only ones you really wanted to talk to,' he remembered slowly. 'You must have been having the same conversation over and over again, but you looked interested in everyone.'

'But people *are* interesting,' said Lizzy, who had never believed that anyone could think otherwise. 'If you made the effort to talk to them, you'd find that out for yourself. It's not that difficult,' she went on bracingly. 'You talked to me, didn't you?'

'It was different with you.'

'Oh, nonsense!' she said. 'How?'

Tye looked at her for a moment, and then away. 'I don't know,' he admitted to the sky outside the window. 'It just was.'

The sound of the engine was very loud in the suddenly constrained silence. Lizzy felt peculiar, as if she had stumbled in the dark and realised that she had lost her way. She wanted to say something flippant, to break the atmosphere with a light-hearted comment, but she couldn't think of anything.

Biting her lip, she looked out of her own window. Below, the red earth stretched out in every direction to a horizon so big it seemed to follow the curve of the earth, but Lizzy didn't see it. The sky reflected only the look in the light grey eyes when Tye had glanced at her, and the echo of his voice drowned out the droning propeller. *It was different with you.*

They had been flying about half an hour when Tye tensed and leant forward to peer more closely out of the window. 'We're over Barra land now,' he said. He sat back almost immediately, but something in his profile made Lizzy's throat tighten absurdly. She looked down, wondering what it was about the land beneath them that meant so much to him.

It was hard to tell much from this height, but the area looked much wilder than the property where she had grown up on the other side of Mathison. It was redder and rockier, the range fissured with gorges and hidden canyons, but as they flew on the hills petered out into the more familiar scrub, broken at intervals by the snaking line of tree-lined creeks.

Tye said nothing more until the plane touched down and bumped along the airstrip that had been cleared in the bush, coming to a halt by a huge boab tree where a brand-new utility truck was waiting in the shade. Lizzy watched the blurring propeller slow until it was turning sluggishly, before it stopped as if overwhelmed by the oppressive silence of the outback.

'I'll get the steps,' said the pilot over his shoulder as he opened his door.

'Don't bother.' Tye unclipped his seatbelt and made his way forward to push open the door on the other side of the plane, impatient to get out and feel his feet firmly back on Barra soil. He climbed out onto the wing and jumped lightly down to the ground.

Lizzy followed more cautiously. She hesitated on the wing, shading her eyes against the glare of the fierce sun as it bounced and glittered on the metal fuselage. Below her, Tye turned and held up his arms.

'Jump,' he said.

And suddenly it seemed quite natural to do as he said.

Lizzy dropped her hands onto his shoulders, and as she jumped she felt his big hands close hard around her waist. He swung her easily down off the wing, but when her feet touched the ground he didn't let her go immediately. Instead he smiled down into her face.

'Welcome to Barra Creek.'

They were standing very close in the sunlight and the silence. Tye's hands were burning through Lizzy's shirt and she was dizzyingly aware of him, of the crease in his cheek and the texture of his skin and the slow, steady pulse beating in his throat that made her body throb in response.

She was still clutching his shoulders. It would be so easy to let her hands slide around his neck, so easy to lean into him, so easy to touch her lips to that tantalising pulse.

So easy to forget just what she was doing here and why.

'The ute's here to take you to the homestead, Mr Gibson,' the pilot interrupted them in a respectful voice, and Lizzy drew a sharp breath and stepped away from Tye, giddy at the thought of how close she had come to making a complete fool of herself again.

Tye's hands fell from her waist and his smile faded. Lizzy had the impression that for a moment he too had forgotten that anyone else was there.

'The ute,' he echoed blankly. 'Oh, yes.'

The pilot had already loaded the plane's cargo, together with Lizzy's case, into the back of the truck. He held the door of the cab open for Lizzy, and she slid into the middle of the bench seat.

'Aren't you coming?' she said to Tye when he made no move to join her.

He was standing by the truck, pulling the tie from his

collar and rolling up his sleeves as if he couldn't wait to shed his urban, entrepreneurial image, looking at the long-remembered land around him almost hungrily.

'No,' he said, bending down to hand her the discarded tie through the window. And Lizzy saw that there was already a subtle change to his expression, as if an intolerable sadness had been eased. 'You go. I think I'd like to walk.'

CHAPTER SIX

THE old homestead stood on rising ground overlooking the creek, surrounded by an oasis of green garden that had been carefully irrigated over the years. The house itself was a low, stone building, with a deep verandah running around it and a corrugated iron roof. There was something solid and dignified about the way it seemed to grow out of the earth, sturdily defying the floods and fire, drought and cyclones that had ravaged the land since it had been built.

Lizzy walked through the rooms, enjoying the cool but finding the atmosphere oddly dispiriting. Everything was immaculately clean but it was clear that Frank Gibson had not been a believer in luxury, or even much comfort.

Perhaps Tye would change that, Lizzy thought. He could certainly afford to bring in a designer and restore the homestead to its past glory. Turning slowly in the big living room, Lizzy narrowed her eyes and imagined how it could be. But it wasn't stylish furniture that Barra needed, she decided. It needed life and laughter and love to banish the lurking ghosts of past Gibsons, all as hard and unforgiving as the land they had claimed as their own.

For want of anything else to do, Lizzy showered and changed into a cool cream dress and peep-toe sandals. As she carefully outlined her mouth with her favourite bold red lipstick, she wondered about Tye and what he was thinking about as he walked back through the bush.

Of course she understood that he had wanted to be on his own, she acknowledged as she blotted her lips, but she couldn't help feeling a little hurt at her abrupt dismissal. She wouldn't have chattered the whole way and spoilt everything for him. She would just have been there to share his pleasure in returning to Barra at last.

But then, Tye wasn't the kind of man who believed in sharing his feelings, Lizzy reminded herself, and for some reason felt depressed.

She made her way out to the verandah, but there was still no sign of him, and after a while Lizzy began to worry. Refusing offers of a drink from the well-trained staff who had been sent up from Sydney, and who appeared to think they were in a luxury hotel rather than a functioning cattle station, she paced up and down the verandah with her arms folded. Every couple of minutes she would stop and check her watch.

Surely he ought to be back by now, she fretted. It would be dark soon. It hadn't been that far from the airstrip. What if he had got lost? Or had fallen and couldn't make it as far as the homestead?

She was about to go and organise a search party when a glimmer of white shirt between the trees down by the creek caught her eye, and a few moments later Tye appeared, looking surprisingly at home even in his city clothes.

'Where have you been?' Lizzy greeted him furiously as he reached the bottom of the verandah steps.

Tye paused with his foot on the first step. 'I came back along the creek,' he said.

'You've been *hours*!'

'I sat for a while,' he said, raising his brows at her tone. 'I was thinking.'

'What about?'

The grey eyes flickered to her face and then away, back towards the great ghost gums lining the creek. 'Things,' he said uninformatively. 'Why, what does it matter?'

'I don't suppose it occurred to you that I might have been worried?' said Lizzy crossly as he came up the last steps to join her on the verandah.

'No,' said Tye. 'I can't say it did. Why would you be worried about me?'

Lizzy found herself unable to answer this. She glowered at him. 'I'm not going to earn my year's salary if you're stumbling around the outback getting lost, am I?'

To her fury, Tye only laughed, as if he were really amused. 'I won't get lost on Barra,' he assured her, and opened the screen door. 'But I'm glad to hear that you're thinking about your bonus! You sit here and think about how you're going to earn it, and when I come back you can tell me about your plans over a drink.'

He disappeared into the house and Lizzy sat in one of the cane chairs, watching the sky deepen from violet to pink to a blaze of red and gold. She wished Tye hadn't laughed like that. How could a mere creasing of the cheeks, a crinkling of eyes and a glimpse of white teeth be enough to leave her feeling winded?

At least she had some time to recover. Lizzy scowled at the sunset and concentrated on getting her breath back. In, out. In, out. In, out. There, no problem.

When Tye reappeared he was wearing moleskin trousers and a pale yellow shirt, and his dark hair was still wet from the shower. Lizzy took one look at him, horrified to find that her mind presented her with a disturbingly vivid picture of him stripping off his clothes and standing naked under the water, and promptly lost control of her breathing again.

Tye was accompanied by a man in a starched jacket whom he introduced as Peter, and whom Lizzy assumed was some kind of butler, although the idea seemed bizarre in the middle of the outback. Perhaps when you were a billionaire you forgot how to answer your own telephone or open your own beer bottle.

'What would you like to drink?' Tye asked her. 'Champagne?'

'No,' said Lizzy quickly. Champagne reminded her too much of Sydney and how he had kissed her down by the harbour. 'I mean…actually I'd prefer a gin and tonic.'

She looked after Peter in some amazement as he vanished noiselessly in search of the drinks. 'Where did you get staff like that?'

'From my Sydney apartment.' Tye sat down in the chair next to hers, very matter-of-fact. 'I sent Peter up with a chef and a housekeeper to get things under control. The pilot won't be based here permanently until I decide how many people I'm going to need.'

'You're making yourself comfortable!'

'I might as well,' said Tye, unperturbed by her dig. 'This is my base now.'

'If you find yourself a wife,' Lizzy reminded him, and his expression hardened.

'I will,' he told her. 'I'm not leaving Barra again.'

Lizzy wondered if he had any idea of what was involved in a marriage. He seemed to think that finding a wife would be a simple process, a question of running his eye over a few suitable candidates and picking out the one he liked best. She thought about pointing out to him that things were likely to prove a little more complicated than that, but there was such grim determination in the set of Tye's jaw that she decided not to bother.

'Where are all these people sleeping?' she asked instead.

'There are several houses left over from my grandparents' days. The manager then had a house, and the governess, people like that.' Tye sounded indifferent. Clearly not a caring, sharing boss, thought Lizzy. He wouldn't spend much time worrying about whether his staff were comfortable or happy as long as they did their jobs.

'And then there's the house my father built for his housekeeper,' he added.

Lizzy looked dubious. 'What does Veronica think about that?' she asked, thinking of Frank Gibson's formidable housekeeper. Veronica had been at Barra for over ten years and had been devoted to Frank.

'It doesn't matter what she thinks,' said Tye coldly. 'She's not here any more.'

'You didn't sack her, did you?' said Lizzy with deep foreboding.

'She sacked herself. I came back to Barra for the first time in twenty years to find myself accused of causing my father's death—although since I was in the States at the time, I'm not quite sure how I was supposed to have done that—and Veronica threatening to walk out the moment I set foot in the homestead.'

Lizzy winced, imagining the scene. It had not been much of a welcome home for him. 'What did you say?'

'That as far as I was concerned the sooner she left, the better.'

'Oh, dear.'

'What was I supposed to do?' Tye demanded irritably. 'Get down on my knees and beg her to stay?'

'You could have tried to get her to listen to your side of the story,' Lizzy suggested. 'She'd been with your father a long time, and she must have been upset at his death. Barra has been her home for a good ten years, and she won't find it easy to get another job. If you'd been able to persuade her to stay it would have done wonders for your reputation. As it is, sacking the locals and importing staff from Sydney isn't going to make you very popular.'

Tye's jaw clenched. 'I haven't sacked anyone,' he said, exasperated. 'Veronica walked out, and if she can't find anywhere to live now, it's not my problem. The station hands are still here. I didn't have a chance to see them when I was here before, but I've been paying their wages, so perhaps they can go into town and tell everyone I'm not, in fact, the devil incarnate!'

They ate that night in a gloomy dining room, sitting at either end of a long polished table. To Lizzy, used to eating basic meals in the big kitchen at home with the station hands and anyone else who happened to be visiting her parents' property, it seemed very odd to be waited on hand and foot. She could only imagine what the chef had thought when he had seen the outback kitchen, but he had managed to prepare an exquisitely presented dinner which was served by Peter, moving soft-footed around the table.

'I wonder how long he'll last,' she said as the door closed behind him. She picked up her fork. 'I give him three weeks at most.'

Tye looked suspiciously down the table. 'What do you mean?'

'Come on, Tye, those guys are used to working in luxury city apartments! They won't think much of conditions out here. What are they going to do with themselves when they're not working? They'll be bored stiff in five minutes, and I don't blame them!'

'They're being extremely well paid,' said Tye, looking down his nose.

Lizzy flourished her fork. 'Money's not everything,' she told him grandly.

'It's why *you're* here.'

It was true, Lizzy acknowledged, subsiding. If it hadn't been for her extravagant taste in shoes and the resulting credit card bill, she wouldn't be here. She wasn't spending two months in the outback for the pleasure of Tye's company, was she?

Was she?

'Isn't it?' insisted Tye.

'Yes,' she muttered.

'I hope you've given some thought to how you're going to earn all this money I've agreed to pay you,' he said with an astringent look.

'I've done some research,' said Lizzy, omitting to mention that her research had taken the form of ringing her mother and enquiring casually about forthcoming events in the area. 'You're in luck. There's a rodeo the weekend after next, and the Mathison races are a couple of weeks later.'

She paused, waiting for Tye to comment positively, but he was unimpressed. 'Is that it?'

'They're both big social occasions,' she pointed out defensively. 'Everyone will be there. The rodeo is an excellent opportunity for me to start introducing you round, and then you can follow up anyone likely at the races. I think it should work well.'

Tye's only response was a noncommittal grunt, so Lizzy ploughed on.

'After you've made some contacts, I thought we could invite everyone to a party here.'

'They won't come.'

'They will once they've had a chance to get to know you properly. Anyway, I bet they're all dying to have a look around Barra. Your father wasn't exactly known for his entertaining, was he? Most people have never been to Barra, and you know how nosy they all are. I'd jump at the opportunity!'

'Not everyone has your enthusiasm for parties,' said Tye, unconvinced.

'They'll want to come to this party, because I'll be spending the next month telling them how brilliant it's going to be,' said Lizzy, warming to her theme. 'I'll organise a fabulous party, the kind of spectacular event that people will talk about for years to come, and we'll invite absolutely everybody.' The blue eyes sparkled with enthusiasm. 'We could fly in a band and entertainers, make it a sort of mini-carnival! It'll be fantastic!'

'How much do you think that's going to cost?' asked Tye dourly.

'Look, what's the point of having all that money if you don't spend it?' she argued. 'It's not even as if it would be an extravagance. As far as you're concerned, I think it would be an *investment*.'

'What would you know about investment?' said Tye nastily. 'It doesn't seem to me that you've got much of a track record in financial management!'

'Maybe not, but I know about people.' Lizzy waved her fork at him. 'I'm telling you, throwing a really generous party and giving everyone a great day out would be the best thing you could do. No one would be able to ignore you after that. You'd get invited back everywhere, and there would be no problem meeting possible Mrs Gibsons.'

'Hmm.'

Disappointed by his lack of enthusiasm, Lizzy put

down her fork. 'You don't sound very keen. I thought you wanted to meet people?'

'I do.'

'So can I go ahead and organise the party or not?'

'All right,' said Tye, but he sounded irritable, and he pushed a prawn morosely around his plate.

Lizzy ruffled up. 'I'm only trying to help.' Talk about ungrateful! Here she was, doing everything he'd asked her to do, and look what thanks she got for it! 'You'll never find a wife unless you're prepared to make an effort.'

'All *right*!' he snapped. 'I've got the point that you want your cash bonus!'

'And the job,' she told him, because she was feeling cross as well by then. 'I quite fancy working in the London office for a while.'

Tye scowled down the table at her. 'You're not going anywhere until I'm married!'

'Why do you think I'm so keen to make a start?' said Lizzy sweetly. No harm in reminding him that her interest in him and his marriage was purely professional. 'The sooner you find a suitable wife, the sooner I can get back to doing what *I* want to do.

'The rodeo's not for a while, so we ought to go into Mathison before then,' she went on, when Tye pointedly failed to congratulate her on her positive attitude. 'People need to get used to seeing you around. There's always someone to meet in the store, and we could drop in at the bank and places like that, to see if anyone is around. The stock agent has a very pretty daughter who's just back from Darwin,' she added. 'I could introduce you to her.'

'Fine,' said Tye.

Lizzy rolled her eyes. It was going to be uphill work

if he was going to be this lukewarm about her ideas. 'What about tomorrow, then?'

'Not tomorrow.' He shook his head definitely. 'I want to have a word with the stockmen and see what state the property is in. I didn't get a chance to look round properly when I was here before.'

'I guess I could start thinking about the party, then,' she said, deflated. It wasn't that she wanted to spend her time with Tye—God forbid!—but it was going to get pretty boring sitting in the homestead all day waiting for him to come back.

Still, it would be fun planning the party. Lizzy perked up a little at the thought. She already had a band in mind, and she would need to book the entertainers. Perhaps they could have a bouncy castle and face painters to keep the children amused? A month wasn't that long, and there was a lot to be done. She had better get on with things.

Lizzy had a solitary breakfast in the dining room the next morning. It was no more cheerful in the morning light, she decided, buttering her toast with a sigh.

Living a life of luxury was all very well, but it was awfully boring. She had wandered along to the kitchen, planning to make herself a cup of coffee and give a hand with the lunch, but her hopes of getting to know the staff had been speedily dashed. The chef, a terrifyingly professional Italian, had ushered her firmly out of the kitchen. Breakfast, she'd been told, would be served in the dining room.

So Lizzy had to sit alone, with nothing to do but drink her coffee and nobody to talk to. There had been no sign of Tye when she woke up. He obviously hadn't been able to wait to get out to his beloved Barra. Clearly the prospect of her company at breakfast was no match for the lure of the bush.

Fine, thought Lizzy, but she couldn't help feeling a little aggrieved. He might at least have waited to see if she wanted to go too.

The screen door slammed just then, and was followed by the sound of angry footsteps ringing on the stone floor in the corridor. Lizzy recognised them instantly as Tye's, and she brightened, excusing the sudden clench of anticipation at the base of her spine on the grounds that while his company might not be just what she wanted, it was better than no company at all.

'There you are!' The door opened abruptly and Tye stood there, wearing jeans and a casual checked shirt but somehow managing to look as dark and formidable and ruthlessly competent as ever.

Lizzy was annoyed to discover that no matter how prepared she thought she was for the sight of him, her heart still did that stupid somersault, soaring gymnastically into her throat before landing—bang!—somewhere in the region of her diaphragm and driving the breath from her lungs.

Tye's face was thunderous, and Lizzy put down her piece of toast with a hand that was suddenly unsteady. 'What's the matter?'

Glacial grey eyes surveyed her sitting in solitary splendour at the breakfast table. Anticipating a day spent making notes or on the phone, Lizzy had put on a sleeveless white top and a fluid, fuchsia-pink skirt, cinched at the waist with a soft purple belt. She looked cool and fresh, but her appearance didn't seem to give Tye any pleasure.

'Did you bring any working clothes with you?' he asked, ignoring her question.

'I've got some jeans for riding. Why?'

'Go and put them on.'

'What, now?'

'You're coming with me,' said Tye grimly.

'But I was going to make some calls about the party this morning,' Lizzy protested.

'The party can wait. We've got more important things to do today. The station hands have all gone!'

Lizzy rolled her eyes. All this fuss just because the men weren't in their quarters. 'They won't have *gone*,' she said, picking up her coffee cup. 'They'll be out mustering or—'

'They're not mustering!' Tye interrupted her with a snarl. 'They've cleared out. And just to make sure I got the message they left a note in their quarters saying that they weren't going to be treated like Veronica, and that I could find myself some stockmen without *principles*.' He practically spat out the word as he strode up and down the dining room, too angry to stand still.

Lizzy put down her coffee. 'Oh, dear,' she said.

He rounded on her furiously. '*Oh, dear?* Is that all you've got to say? I don't know how long they've been gone, or if they did anything before they left. And if they're in town stirring up trouble with Veronica, I'm not going to be able to find anyone to replace them quickly.'

Lizzy let him stomp around, swearing fluently, and waited until he had got the worst of it off his chest. She didn't underestimate the seriousness of his predicament. A station the size of Barra couldn't operate without stockmen. Even if Tye could persuade local contractors to come in at this stage of the season, he still needed someone to help maintain the property on a day-to-day basis. There was just too much for one man to cover.

'What are you going to do?' she asked when he had run out of invective.

'I can tell you one thing I'm *not* going to do, and that's sit around wringing my hands and saying "Oh, dear",' Tye replied savagely. 'If they think I'm going to slink back to Sydney because nobody likes me, they've got another think coming! I'll manage somehow, even if I have to muster every single paddock by myself.'

'Right,' said Lizzy, knowing quite well how impossible that would be.

'I'll see if I can find some more men tomorrow, but first we've got to see what kind of state things are in. It could be a couple of weeks since anyone has checked the licks or the watering points.'

'We?' she asked delicately.

Tye had been muttering to himself, but he swung round at Lizzy's interruption. 'You and me,' he said. 'Who else is there?'

'Well, you have got three other men here, as well as a housekeeper,' she pointed out.

'The pilot left first thing this morning to bring in more equipment from the Sydney office, and how much use do you think those others are going to be? They wouldn't know a bull from a bowl of soup! You grew up on a station. At least you know what you're looking at.'

'Well, yes, but—'

'You're all I've got, Lizzy,' Tye interrupted her before she could refuse. 'I need you.'

I need you. The words hung, echoing in the air. Lizzy saw his mouth twist as he heard himself admit that he couldn't manage on his own, and she felt suddenly ashamed. He had already begged for her help once. She didn't need to make him do it again.

Gulping a last mouthful of coffee, she put down her cup as she got to her feet, taking the rest of her toast with her. 'I'll go and change,' she said.

There were horses corralled in the homestead paddock, but they took the ute to cover the ground more quickly. Tye drove with a kind of cold, controlled rage, his knuckles white on the steering wheel as the vehicle juddered over the corrugations and left a cloud of red dust billowing behind them.

Lizzy braced herself against the dashboard and opted for silence. Small talk wasn't an option as they jolted and lurched furiously across the vast paddocks, even if Tye had been in the mood.

Barra was in a bad way. Fences were down, dams crumbling, and water points leaking uselessly into the ground. Old oil drums which should have been filled with extra nutrients for the cattle to lick were empty. Tye let one drop with an exclamation of disgust.

'The one thing I can say about my father is that he would never have neglected Barra,' he said. 'Those men can't have done any work since he fell ill. So much for their principles!' he added contemptuously. He surveyed the land with a bleak expression. 'I never thought things would be as bad as this,' he admitted, as if the words had been wrung from him.

It must be a bitter moment for him, thought Lizzy, to find his dream crumbling and neglected. She tried to encourage him, going to stand next to him. 'They could be worse.'

'Excellent. Fatuous clichés!' he growled sarcastically. 'That's all I need!'

The blue eyes snapped dangerously. 'Look, it's not

my fault you've got such a rotten reputation no one wants to work for you!'

They glared at each other for a moment, before Tye took off his hat and ran his fingers through his hair. 'No, I know,' he admitted heavily. 'I'm sorry. I'm just...'

'I know,' said Lizzy, her spurt of temper evaporating as quickly as it had erupted. Apologies didn't come to him any more easily than begging did, and although she should have been pleased, she found that she wasn't enjoying his discomfort. 'It's disappointing,' she said, to help him out, although the word seemed inadequate to describe Tye's feelings.

'Yes.' There was a flicker of gratitude in the glance Tye sent her. 'I wasn't banking on having to start from scratch. There are fifteen thousand cattle out there,' he said, gesturing around him. 'They all need to be mustered in. But even if I could handle them all myself there isn't any point until the yards have been repaired and there are some decent fences, not to mention gates that will close. We're already weeks into the season,' he went on morosely, jamming his hat back on his head, 'and it could take weeks to find experienced men who are prepared to work for me. What am I going to do in the meantime?'

'We could fix a lot of it ourselves,' Lizzy heard herself say, and he turned to stare at her, as surprised as she was.

'We?' he said, just as she had said earlier that morning in the dining room.

'You and me,' she said, consciously echoing his own words. 'You were the one who pointed out that I grew up on a station,' she went on with a trace of impatience when he hesitated. 'I might not be a man, but I'm better than nothing, aren't I?'

'You're a lot better than that,' said Tye slowly, his eyes on her face, vivid beneath her hat, the blue eyes bright with determination and her chin tilted at a stubborn angle.

'Well, then.' Lizzy brushed her hands together as if the matter were already decided.

'It would be a lot of hard work,' he warned her.

'You think I've never mended a fence before?' she retorted. 'Dad used to make us help at home. He insisted that Ellie and I could do everything that our brother did, and as soon as we could ride we'd go out with him. I'm not just a pretty face, you know.'

Something that was not quite a smile deepened the creases in Tye's cheeks. 'Oh, I know that,' he said, an oddly disquieting undercurrent of amusement in his voice. 'I just thought you were someone who'd rather be painting your nails than getting your hands dirty.'

'Normally I would,' said Lizzy, 'but I don't mind when I have to.'

'But you *don't* have to,' Tye pointed out. 'You're here as a social secretary, not a station hand. Mending fences wasn't part of our agreement.'

'Well, I know, but there's no reason why I shouldn't help.' She looked at him, puzzled by his reluctance to accept her offer. 'Don't you want me to?'

'It's not that,' he said. 'I'm just wondering why you would.'

Lizzy wondered herself. What was she doing, offering herself for the most boring and backbreaking chores on a station? Her mind shied away from one possible answer, which was that she couldn't bear the look of defeat in the eyes of a man who had proved himself to be ruthless and arrogant and callously unconcerned about the feelings of anyone else.

'You're paying me a lot of money,' she muttered, opting for another, less disturbing answer. 'My PR skills aren't going to be much in demand while you're busy out here, so I might as well make myself useful. Besides,' she went on, getting onto safer ground, 'I'd go mad sitting around in the homestead all day. You're obviously not going to have time to do anything about your social life until you've got the station under control. You might find some men looking for work at the rodeo, but that's not for a couple of weeks, and we could at least make a start until then.'

'OK.' All at once the rigidity went out of Tye's shoulders and he smiled at her. 'Let's do it.'

'Great.'

Lizzy tried to sound matter-of-fact, but inwardly she was dismayed at the thrill that ran through her. It wasn't just his smile, although that was having its by now predictable effect on her heart, which was performing handsprings that any gymnast would be proud of.

No, it was something to do with the fact that she was going to be spending the next two weeks getting hot and dirty and tired, and not really caring because she would be with Tye.

Uh-oh, Lizzy thought as alarm bells rang belatedly in her brain.

Hadn't she already decided that getting involved with Tye would be a very bad idea? That the only way she would get through the next two months was to keep their relationship strictly professional? And wasn't committing herself to working alone with him under the big outback sky the very *last* way to do that?

Still, it was too late to back out now, Lizzy told herself. And she *would* be bored if she was left on her own.

She wasn't going to do anything silly. She was just going to mend fences.

As she turned to get back into the ute, Tye put out a hand to stop her. 'Lizzy?'

'Yes?'

'Thanks.'

He didn't say anything else, just got into the ute, put it into gear and drove on, but it was enough to make the blood sing through Lizzy's veins. She sat smiling ridiculously beside him until she realised what she was doing and forced the corners of her mouth to turn down. She wasn't going to do anything silly, she reminded herself sternly.

Was she?

CHAPTER SEVEN

THEY began in the yards that afternoon, and it took them another five days of solid work before they had straightened all the wobbly posts and replaced the broken rails.

'Do you think it'll do?' asked Lizzy, swinging the last gate experimentally.

Tye took off his hat and wiped his forehead with the back of his arm. 'I reckon.'

Together they surveyed the expanse of wooden pens with pride. The yards looked a lot better now than they had done five days previously, and although the work had been just as hard as Tye had warned, Lizzy had found it surprisingly satisfying. She was dying to see them in use.

'Perhaps we should muster a few cattle and draft them through,' she suggested. 'Just as a practice, to make sure we haven't missed any gaps?' She glanced hopefully at Tye and stopped abruptly. 'Why are you looking at me like that?'

He grinned. 'I was just remembering you at your sister's wedding. I would never have guessed then that anyone who wore shoes like that could be quite so excited about a few empty pens!'

'It's funny, isn't it?' Lizzy ran her hand thoughtfully along the top bar of the gate. 'If you'd asked me a month ago if I'd like to spend five days repairing cattle yards, I'd have said absolutely not. I'd have opted firmly to stay in my nice clean office, where I could wear my nice shoes and not have to worry about chipping my nail polish.'

She held out her hands before her and inspected her torn and grubby nails with a rueful smile. 'I used to grumble like mad when Dad sent me out on repairs, and I thought I never wanted to do that kind of thing again, but this time I've really enjoyed it.'

'You've done a good job,' said Tye. 'Your father would be proud of you. You're a hard worker.'

Lizzy slid a glance at him from under her lashes. 'Did you think I wouldn't be?'

'No, but I wouldn't have blamed you if you'd given up after the first day.'

'What, and miss all the fun?'

'I don't think there's been much of that,' he said, thinking of the hours they had spent patching and sawing and hammering in the sun without a break.

'Oh, I don't know about that.' Lizzy pretended to consider the matter. 'What about that time you bashed your thumb and then dropped the hammer on your toe?'

'Glad you enjoyed the show,' said Tye dryly.

'The script might need to be edited for a family audience,' she teased him, remembering his colourful language as he'd hopped around the pen, 'but otherwise it was very...expressive!'

He laughed. Yes, there went her heart, thought Lizzy, resigned, cavorting around her chest like a kangaroo.

'I hadn't used a hammer in years,' he defended himself, unaware of Lizzy's efforts to reinflate her lungs and get her breathing under control.

'I guess at GCS you've got use. to having someone to do your hammering for you,' she managed a little unevenly.

'I guess so.' Tye's smile faded and he leant on the

rail with a thoughtful expression. 'You know, when I imagined myself back at Barra, I never thought I'd be doing this kind of stuff,' he confessed. 'I had a vision of myself riding around, inspecting the herd but leaving all the dirty work to someone else. I'm kind of glad it didn't work out that way. Repairing these yards, building something real…it's been a good feeling. It's a long time since I've done anything like this.'

'You built up GCS,' Lizzy reminded him. 'That's real.'

He looked out over the yards. 'Is it?'

'I bet it feels pretty real to all those people you employ, and to those millions around the world who use GCS technology every day.' She turned round so that she could lean back against the rail beside him. 'And what about those dollars in your bank account? Don't they feel real?'

'It's not the same,' said Tye stubbornly. 'I don't regret anything I've done. Building up a company like GCS is a challenge, and the higher the stakes you play for, the more exciting it is. But it's not like making something concrete. I'd forgotten what it's like to do something with my hands.'

Out of the corner of her eye, Lizzy saw him turn his hands over and study them. They were brown and dusty, with strong wrists and long, blunt fingers, and the memory of how they had felt against her skin shuddered without warning down her spine.

'It's a good feeling,' said Tye.

If only he knew.

Lizzy straightened abruptly away from him. 'Lunch will be ready,' she said. 'We'd better go back.'

They carried the tools back to the ute, and slung them

into the back. Tye got into the driver's seat, but he didn't start the engine immediately.

'I've been thinking,' he said, but almost as if the words had been forced out of him.

'What about?'

'About that job you wanted to do.'

Lizzy frowned, reviewing the list of jobs ahead. She couldn't remember expressing any preference for any of them. Unless Tye meant a trial muster? 'Which one?' she asked, puzzled.

'The one in London.'

It took a few moments for her to work out that he was talking about the plum posting he had offered her as an incentive to find him a suitable wife. The agreement they had made seemed like something that had happened in another life. Taken up with the work in the yards, Lizzy had forgotten just what she was doing at Barra Creek.

Clearly Tye hadn't.

'Oh, yes,' she said flatly. 'That job.'

'It's yours.'

Lizzy had been staring straight ahead, but at that she swivelled in her seat and looked at him blankly. 'What?'

'When all this is over, you can go to London.'

'What about your marriage?' she made herself ask.

'I still need that to go ahead.' Tye sounded as if he were having to convince himself. 'And the extra money I promised is dependent on me getting married before June, but you can have the job whatever happens.' He glanced at Lizzy's amazed face and then back at the steering wheel. 'I reckon you've earned it. You've worked really hard over the last few days, and it's not what you came here to do.'

Lizzy knew that she ought to be thrilled, but all at

once it was hard to feel very excited about the thought
of leaving Barra and taking up a job in a strange city.

'You said you wanted to work in London,' he reminded her when she didn't say anything. 'You could
go over and enjoy their summer.'

He obviously couldn't wait to get rid of her.

'Great.' Lizzy forced a smile. 'Thanks.'

It was just as well Tye had reminded her about the
real purpose of her presence at Barra, she told herself as
she lay in bed that night. She had almost forgotten and
that would never do.

Staring up at the ceiling in the dark, Lizzy struggled
to remember how reluctant she had been to come to
Barra and how she had needed to talk herself into taking
the bizarre job Tye had offered her. Her reasons were
still the same, she reminded herself, just as Tye's were.
They might have found it surprisingly easy to get on
when they were working together in the yards, but that
didn't mean that anything had changed.

Tye still needed a wife, and it was still her job to find
him one. She had better keep that firmly in mind.

But as the days passed, Lizzy found it harder and
harder to remember. Afterwards, when she looked back
at that time, she was amazed at how naturally they'd
fallen into a routine. Every day they got up at five, so
that they were ready to leave at dawn. Reluctant to waste
time coming back to the homestead at midday, they took
sandwiches with them, and at midday they would make
a fire and boil a billy for tea.

About five, they headed for home, their muscles aching and their skin gritty with dust and dirt. Arriving back
hot and thirsty, they shared a cold beer on the verandah
before they went inside for a shower, and every time

Lizzy thought it was the best thing that she had ever tasted.

The shower always felt pretty good, too. Lizzy made a point of changing into a dress, but every night when she looked in the mirror her reflection looked more and more strange. Was that really her, that woman with the bold lipstick and the absurd shoes? She would hear her heels clicking on the stone floor as she walked along to the dining room, and marvel that only weeks ago she had worn shoes like those all day.

Frustrated by their insistence on simple sandwiches for lunch, the chef put all his artistry into preparing exquisite evening meals whose delicacy Lizzy was too tired and hungry to appreciate. She had always been a gourmet, much mocked by her family for her culinary pretensions, but now she found herself longing for a plain steak or a roast instead of the elaborate concoctions that appeared on the table.

Lizzy worked harder in those ten days than she had ever worked before. Stepping out of the shower each day, she caught sight of herself in the mirror and realised that the physical exercise was making her leaner and fitter. Perhaps that was why she felt so alert and alive, and it was nothing whatsoever to do with the fact that Tye was always there, settling his hat on his head, squinting at the horizon, smiling his smile.

Perhaps it was the reason why, in spite of growing up in the outback, she felt as if she were experiencing it for the very first time. It was as if she had never before seen the pink and grey galahs wheeling out of the trees in perfect formation, never watched brolgas dancing their slow, stately dance, or been stirred by the wild beauty of brumbies running free. As if she had never smelt the dry earth, or the air at dawn, or spinifex grass warming in the sun.

Every day they discovered more problems. They had only got as far as the home paddocks, themselves huge fenced areas that ringed the homestead, and sometimes Lizzy would look out towards the ranges and think of the hundreds of square miles that were still to be checked. She worried that the season would be over before Tye got a chance to muster.

There was so much that needed to be done, but whenever she mentioned it to Tye he told her that they would just have to take things a step at a time. Lizzy was secretly amazed that he could seem so relaxed. It was hard to believe sometimes that this was the same man as the dark, sardonic stranger who had walked into Ellie's wedding. Day by day, the guarded look faded from his face. The harsh lines softened, the cynical twist vanished from his mouth, the watchfulness from his eyes.

Lizzy sat one day watching him as he crouched by the fire, poking the embers to stoke up a flame under the billy. His jeans were dusty, his shirt rolled up to reveal the strong forearms. His hat was tilted forward, shadowing his eyes, but the sunlight banded the lower half of his face and she could see that the corners of his mouth were turned up. He didn't look like a ruthless tycoon any more. He looked younger, more carefree.

He looked happy.

Something twisted inside Lizzy, and she must have made an involuntary movement for Tye looked up, his eyes as startlingly light and as penetrating as ever, even in the shade of his hat.

'What?' he asked.

'Nothing,' said Lizzy quickly, casting around with a

hint of desperation. 'I was just thinking what a beautiful place this is,' she lied.

Tye looked around him. They had stopped for lunch by a small creek. During the wet season it would be churning with turbulent water, but it had already been dry for weeks, and the stony bed was littered with broken branches that had been carried down and abandoned by the torrent and were now bleaching in sun.

The watercourse was lined with gnarled and knobbled gums. Beneath their smooth branches, the ground was covered with great curls of silvery bark that had peeled away and fallen to join the carpet of dried leaves whose scent drifted in the sunlight. It was very quiet.

'I remember coming here once with my mother,' he said slowly, turning back to the fire. 'We had a picnic.'

It was the first time he had mentioned his childhood. Lizzy hadn't liked to ask in case he didn't want to talk about it, but now that he had brought the subject up himself, she couldn't resist the chance to find out more. 'What was she like?' she asked curiously.

'My mother?' Hunkered down by the fire, Tye poked at it as he considered the question. 'She was very pretty, very frivolous, and completely unsuited to life in the outback. She came out from England on a visit, and had a ridiculously romantic idea about life on a cattle station. She and my father got married after a whirlwind courtship, and the initial attraction didn't last long when faced with the reality of the silence and the heat and the isolation.'

He poked the embers reflectively. 'It's surprising, really, that she lasted as long as she did. She stuck it out for eight years, then she decided that she couldn't stand it any longer and went back to England. I was seven when she left.'

Tye sounded matter-of-fact, but Lizzy's heart cracked at the thought of the lonely little boy who had been abandoned by his mother to a bullying father.

'I don't understand how she could do that!' she said, wondering why Tye seemed to have reserved all his bitterness for his father, and not for the mother who had left him when he needed her most. 'Why didn't she take you with her?'

He shrugged carelessly. 'She knew that I belonged at Barra even then. I would have been miserable in England. I went to see her a few years ago, before she died. She'd married again, and was much happier this time. She needed people, my mother. No wonder she was miserable in the outback! Barra must have seemed like a bad dream to her. She was in her element at a party, and when she wasn't socialising she was shopping or having lunch with a friend.'

Lizzy crushed a handful of leaves between her fingers. 'She sounds a bit like me,' she said uncomfortably.

Tye looked at her. She was leaning against a fallen tree trunk in the shade, long legs sprawled out in front of her, hat on the ground beside her. The thick blonde hair was flattened where it had been jammed on her head, and there were streaks of dust on her face. Her gaze was blue and warm and faintly troubled, but the wide mouth still tilted irrepressibly upwards.

'No,' he said, 'my mother wasn't anything like you.'

Somewhat reassured, Lizzy watched him as he used the stick to lift the lid of the billy and check whether the water was boiling. 'Why did she marry your father if she was so sociable? She must have known it would be lonely out here.'

'She convinced herself that it was a grand passion, and that that would be enough.' The grey eyes held a familiar sardonic gleam as Tye glanced at Lizzy again. 'She soon learnt that it wasn't. My father loved her in his way, but he was pathologically jealous and he made her life a misery. It doesn't take much for a grand passion to tip over into obsession, and love like that is destructive.'

He sounded as if he were warning her. Lizzy's eyes slid away and she let the crumbled leaves drift through her fingers. 'No wonder you don't believe in love with parents like that.'

'Who says that I don't believe in love?'

'Do you?'

'Sure,' said Tye, lifting the billy off the fire and pouring the tea into two battered enamel mugs. 'I just don't believe that it lasts.'

Lizzy took the mug he handed her. 'Never?' she asked.

'Not in my experience.' Tye sat down on a log and leant forward, holding the mug between his knees.

On the ground at his feet, Lizzy was achingly conscious of how near he was. All she would have to do would be to lean a little sideways and she could rest her cheek against his thigh. And then—if he wanted to—he would be able to tangle his fingers in her hair, maybe even stroke the nape of her neck.

Lizzy caught her breath as a tiny shiver slithered down her spine, and made herself shift away from him. She stared at his scuffed and dusty boots, now safely out of reach. 'So you've never fallen in love and thought that it would last for ever?'

She thought at first that he wouldn't answer. 'Once,' he admitted at last.

'What was her name?'

'Sasha.' Tye rolled the name around his mouth as if

tasting the memory. 'She was beautiful, the kind of girl men fantasise about, but she was more than that. Bewitching is the only word I can think of. Her hair was long and black, like silk, and her eyes were the greenest green I've ever seen, and when she smiled...' He paused, and stared unseeingly across the creek. 'When she smiled, all you could think about was how much you wanted her.'

Acutely conscious of her own short blonde hair and eyes that were not even a vaguely greenish shade, Lizzy scowled into her tea. She had only asked for a name, not a detailed description. She wished that she hadn't asked now. Tye was still raving on about Sasha and how beautiful and alluring and irresistible she had been.

'I was crazy about her,' he said unnecessarily. 'I left home swearing that I would never get married, but I asked Sasha to marry me the day I met her.'

'That was a bit romantic for you, wasn't it?' said Lizzy, sounding peeved.

'I was crazy about her,' he said unnecessarily. 'We couldn't get enough of each other. Sasha was my first real love, and I really thought that she would be my only one. It was my own grand passion!' he added in a self-mocking tone.

'So how long did this *grand passion* last?' asked Lizzy, unaccountably peeved.

'Until I made the mistake of losing all my money.' Tye drank some tea, apparently unmoved by the memory. 'My first company collapsed a couple of months after we met and I lost all my assets—including Sasha.'

'But that's awful!' said Lizzy, horrified. 'You mean she was only interested in your money after all?'

He glanced down at her, a hint of amusement in his face. 'Don't sound so shocked! You don't get near girls like Sasha unless you play in the big league. They're not about sitting at home being supportive when things go wrong. They're about showing the world that you've made it. Sasha liked me, I'm sure, but only as long as I was what's known as a High Net Worth Individual.'

'Weren't you bitter when she dumped you?' Lizzy couldn't help asking, although she wasn't really sure she wanted to know the answer.

'Oh, I ranted and raved for a week or so,' said Tye, curling his lip contemptuously at the memory of his younger self, 'and then I set about making my fortune again. Sasha taught me a valuable lesson and I had to learn it some time. It might as well have been her that taught me as anyone else.'

Lizzy turned back to face the creek and picked up another handful of leaves. 'You can't say that love doesn't last just because you've had one bad experience,' she said carefully. 'We're not all like Sasha.'

'Even nice girls change their minds,' he pointed out. 'You broke off your engagement, just like Sasha did.'

'That was different!' Lizzy protested. 'I wasn't pretending to be in love with Stephen for what I could get out of him! I did love him. He's kind, considerate, sensitive and great company—all things I want in a man—but I didn't love him enough or in the right way.'

Crushing the leaves in her fingers, she lifted them to her nose and breathed in the dry, distinctive fragrance of the bush. 'When I fall in love, *really* in love, I won't change my mind,' she told Tye defiantly. 'When I fall in love it will be for ever.'

She felt rather than saw him shake his head. 'You'd better fall in love with someone who feels the same,' he warned her, 'or you're going to end up disappointed.'

Lizzy looked down at the leaves in her hand and tried

to picture the ideal man who would walk into her life one day and make everything right, but all she could see was Tye's dark, severe face with his disconcerting eyes and heart-shaking smile.

There was no point in even *thinking* about falling in love with him. Lizzy brushed the leaves briskly from her hands, and with them the mere idea. Even if Tye hadn't already made it very plain that love was never going to be on his agenda, he was nothing like her ideal. She needed to do just as he said, and fall in love with someone who was capable of feeling the same way about her.

'I will,' she said, and it was only afterwards that she wondered whether she might have sounded a lot less sure than she should have done.

'Ouch!' Lizzy dropped the wire and whipped her hand to her mouth.

Tye looked up sharply. 'What have you done?' he demanded in quick concern.

'Caught my thumb on the barbed wire,' she mumbled, intent on sucking the wound.

'Let me see.' He pulled her hand from her mouth and held it between both of his as he inspected the tear which ran along her thumb and down towards her wrist. It wasn't deep, but it looked red and angry, and blood was still welling. He frowned. 'You should have been wearing gloves. That looks sore.'

'It's OK.' His hands were cool and competent, and Lizzy was burningly aware of his fingertips touching her skin. Pulling her hand away, she bent to pick up the wire again, only to find herself pushed aside by an exasperated Tye.

'Here, I'll do that.' He finished attaching the barbed wire to the post while Lizzy stood sucking the side of her thumb and watching him with a shade of resentment. She had been struggling with that wretched barbed wire all day, and Tye made it look so easy.

When he had done, Tye tossed the tools into the back of the ute. Lizzy took her thumb out of her mouth. 'We haven't finished,' she said in surprise.

'We have for today.'

'But it's only three o'clock!'

Tye held the passenger door open for her. 'It's Saturday,' he said. 'You've been working for ten days without a break. I think you could have the rest of the afternoon off.'

'What are you going to do?' asked Lizzy a little ungraciously as she climbed up into the cab.

'I'm going to make sure that wound of yours is clean,' he told her, getting in beside her, 'and then I'm going to do something I've been meaning to do ever since I got back.'

She nodded, thinking that it was about time that Tye rang his headquarters. 'They must be going frantic in Sydney waiting to hear from you.' After the evening meal, he would disappear into his office to send e-mails, but there was a limit to how much could be done electronically when everyone else had gone home.

'It's the weekend,' Tye reminded her. 'There's no point in ringing anyone today, and anyway, I don't want to. I've got a better idea.'

He looked sideways at Lizzy and smiled suddenly at her puzzled expression, his eyes alight with a blithe, breathtaking charm. 'How do you fancy a swim?' he asked.

'Are you sure you know where you're going?' Lizzy asked about an hour later.

They were picking their way through scrub that seemed to be getting thicker and thicker. It was very hot and the silence was crushing.

They'd left the ute by the track. Casually, Tye had taken her good hand and headed off between the spindly gum trees, and although Lizzy could easily have pulled away, it had seemed silly to make a fuss.

She was excruciatingly aware of his fingers around hers, but there was nothing lover-like about the way Tye was holding her hand, she reasoned. He was intent on his surroundings and had probably forgotten that she was there at all, which was another reason for checking that they weren't about to get lost in the middle of the bush.

'Quite sure,' said Tye, ducking beneath a branch. 'This is old country, and it's not going to change in twenty years. We're almost there.'

Sure enough, the dry, dusty scrub was already giving way to weathered rocks, and they emerged a few moments later beside a waterhole so beautiful and unexpected that Lizzy gasped. Hidden between the red rocks, the water had pooled deep and clear. The surface was mirror-still, reflecting back the deep blue of the sky and the perfect outlines of the silvery gums that leant out over its depths.

'Oh,' said Lizzy on a long breath.

Tye nodded, pleased by her reaction. 'I spent a lot of time here as a kid,' he said. 'I always think of it as my secret place.'

As if suddenly becoming aware that he was still holding her hand, he let it go. Pretending that she hadn't noticed, Lizzy crouched on the edge and dipped her fingers into the water, spreading her fingers in its silky coolness. The cold stung the cut on her thumb, but not enough to spoil her pleasure in the scene. The slightest of movements was enough to set the light rocking, and tiny shadows rippled over her skin.

'It's beautiful,' she said, looking up at Tye with a smile as she withdrew her hands and flicked the water from her fingers, the droplets spinning and sparkling in the glittering sunlight.

'Yes,' he agreed without taking his eyes from her face. 'It is.'

Lizzy's smile faded as the air evaporated between them. She was very conscious of her wet hands, of the dazzling light, of the beating heat and the silence that stretched around them. Without being aware of what she was doing, she straightened.

Tye drew a breath. He seemed about to take a step towards her when at the last second he changed his mind and swung away. 'Come on, let's swim,' he said gruffly.

He pulled his T-shirt over his head, and Lizzy swallowed at the sight of his lean, powerful body. She could see the muscles in his flat stomach, the dark hair on his chest, the flex of his broad shoulders, and desire slammed into her with such force that her knees gave way and she collapsed onto a rock.

Bending her head, pretending to fumble with her shoes, Lizzy fought the wave of dizziness. Her eyes cast down, she could see only his bare feet on the warm red rock, but her imagination was already filling in the rest of him, travelling up the long, straight legs, over the economical hips and iron-hard stomach where it disappeared into the khaki shorts...

Lizzy jerked her head up with a sharp intake of breath. Anyone would think that she had never seen a man's body before!

It took her ages to unbutton her shirt. Her fingers felt clumsy and uncoordinated, and she was having trouble concentrating with Tye standing there watching her, wearing only his shorts. Eventually she managed to peel off her shirt, only to face the challenge of standing up to take her shorts off.

She felt desperately exposed when she was finally ready, and all she wanted to do was scramble back into her clothes again. There was absolutely nothing indecent about her turquoise swimsuit, but under Tye's light gaze she might as well have been naked. Holding in her stomach and avoiding his eyes, she made a big thing of dipping her toe into the water.

'It's cold,' she said.

'It's no good tiptoeing round on the edge like that,' said Tye. 'You have to jump in.' He pointed to a rock further up. 'It's deep there.'

He took the boulders in a couple of easy bounds before he stopped to look back at Lizzy, still hesitating below him. 'Aren't you coming?'

She looked up at him, torn by a terrible desire to go with him and fear of what might happen if he so much as brushed against her. She wouldn't be able to resist if he touched her. Already she could feel her control spooling away. It would be so easy to give in to temptation and burrow in that hard body, to throw herself into his arms and beg him to make love to her.

To make a complete fool of herself, in fact.

'What's the problem?' he called down to her.

You. Your bare chest and your bare legs and your arms and your shoulders and your hands and your mouth...

She couldn't say that, though, could she?

'What about crocs?' she asked in a wavering voice, hoping that he would think that she was shaking from fear and not from desire.

'There weren't any twenty years ago, and there won't be any now,' he told her. 'Stop making excuses and come up here!'

She climbed up carefully, so that she didn't need to take his hand. At the top, she averted her eyes from him and peered over the edge instead. It looked a much bigger drop than it had from down below. At least it gave her something else to be nervous about.

'Are you sure this is a good idea?' she said.

'Yes,' said Tye, uncompromising as ever. He stood on the edge beside her, tall and solid and etched in diamond clarity against the blue sky. He stretched out an arm. 'Give me your hand.'

Of course she shouldn't. She should say that she didn't really want to swim. She should scramble back down the rocks and into her clothes and out of danger.

But Lizzy didn't do it. She put her hand out and felt his close tightly around it. One touch and her nerves steadied, her doubts vanished, and she was suddenly, gloriously glad to be alive.

'We'll jump together,' said Tye. 'Are you ready?'

'Yes.'

'One...two...'

'Three!' Lizzy yelled with a mixture of elation and terror as they leapt off the rock hand in hand. There was a moment of weightlessness, just the two of them suspended together in the dazzling light, and then they plunged into the clear water.

It closed over Lizzy's head and Tye lost his grip on her hand as she disappeared beneath the surface. It was very cold, so cold that she was gasping for breath as she emerged, shaking the hair out of her eyes and laughing with sheer exhilaration.

Treading water, she looked around for Tye, and he

popped up beside her, his hair plastered to his head like a seal and his eyes almost silver in the sunlight between dark, spiky lashes. He was laughing, too, his teeth strong and white against his tanned skin, and as he slicked his wet hair back from his face, Lizzy's heart seemed to stop.

It's the shock of the cold water, she told herself, but she knew that it wasn't. It wasn't anything to do with her torn thumb throbbing, either. It was knowing that a single stroke would take her to him. She could wind herself around him, run her hands over his broad brown back and taste his wet skin... Lizzy could feel herself unravelling and she ducked below the water again, forcing herself to swim in the other direction.

OK, so it wasn't the cold water. It was plain, old-fashioned, uncomplicated lust. Lizzy splashed around, pretending to have a good time, grimly reminding herself of the realities of her situation. Tye was single-minded, cynical, selfish. He cared only about Barra. Letting herself get any more involved with him than she already was would be asking for trouble.

It was only a physical attraction, anyway, Lizzy decided. She would just have to ignore it and get on with what she had come here to do.

No problem.

CHAPTER EIGHT

IT WAS too cold to stay in the water for long. Lizzy watched with trepidation as Tye hauled himself out onto the rocks. Drawing a sharp, shuddering breath at the sight of the water streaming down the backs of his thighs, she looked around for an easier way to get out. She wanted a gently shelving beach so that she could sidle out and make a grab for her clothes.

Lizzy swam hopefully along the edge, but it was soon obvious that unless she wanted to freeze to death she would have to take the hand Tye was reaching down to her. He pulled her effortlessly out of the water in one fluid movement, but she landed unevenly and stumbled against him. The touch of his bare, wet skin was electrifying, and Lizzy flinched away as if from a shock.

She was just going to ignore the gut-wrenching twist of desire. Wasn't that what she'd decided? No problem, she had told herself.

'You're trembling,' said Tye.

Lizzy avoided his eyes. 'I'm cold,' she muttered, wrapping her arms around herself and wondering how it was possible to feel so cold on the outside while inside you were on fire.

'Sit in the sun for a minute. You'll soon warm up.'

Warming up was the last thing she needed, thought Lizzy, but she lay down on a flat rock that had absorbed the heat of the day and was worn smooth by aeons of time. She flung an arm across her eyes, as if to protect them from the glare of the sun but really to block out the sight of Tye stretching out beside her, and concentrated on taking deep, slow breaths.

Ignore the booming of her pulse. Ignore the hollow feeling in her stomach. Ignore the nerves twitching with awareness under her skin. No problem.

The sun beat down, bouncing off the rocks around them. Lizzy had stopped shivering, but without the sound of her chattering teeth the silence was oppressive. She had to think of something to say, something that would convince Tye, not to mention herself, that she hadn't forgotten why she was there, that she was in no danger *at all* of mistaking the enforced intimacy of the last few days when they had been working together for anything else.

In the end, though, it was Tye who spoke first. 'If we finish that fence tomorrow, we should be able to move onto the next paddock,' he said.

Peeking at him from under her arm, Lizzy saw that he was shifting his shoulders to settle himself more comfortably against the rock. He was obviously following his own train of thought, she noted, obscurely piqued by his ability to look so relaxed. Whatever he had been thinking about, it clearly *wasn't* about her or the fact that she was lying next to him practically naked.

'We could do something about that drinking trough in there,' he went on, 'and—'

'Tomorrow's Sunday,' she interrupted him, more sharply than she had intended. She might have known that he would be thinking about his precious property. If she had to lie here wrestling with desire, the least Tye could do was sound as if he were having to make some effort to control himself too!

'So?' Tye asked lazily. He lifted his head to look at

her, and Lizzy quickly dropped her arm back over her eyes.

'So there's the rodeo in Mathison,' she told him. 'You still want a wife, don't you?'

There was a tiny pause. 'Yes,' said Tye.

'We ought to go. Everyone will be there and it will be a good chance for you to meet people.' Lizzy hoped that she sounded suitably cheerful at the prospect. It wouldn't do for Tye to guess that she would much rather be mending the drinking trough.

'I guess I should find out exactly what you're looking for,' she ploughed on, glad of the arm that must hide most of her expression. 'I don't want to waste time introducing you to redheads if you definitely prefer brunettes, for instance. Have you given any thought to the kind of girl you'd like to marry?'

'It's funny you should say that,' said Tye, 'because I've been thinking about it a lot, and I know *exactly* what I want.'

'Oh.' Lizzy was disconcerted, and even a little put out. All that time she'd been slaving away over his fences, and he'd been calming considering the kind of wife he'd like! 'Well, that should make my life easier,' she said, determinedly bright.

'I hope so.'

She stiffened slightly at the undercurrent of amusement she detected in his voice. 'What *do* you want?'

She heard Tye move beside her. She couldn't see him, but she could feel that he was leaning up on one elbow, looking down at her.

'I don't think it would be a good idea to have anyone too young,' he said. 'Big age gaps are always difficult, aren't they? I was thinking that someone in her thirties would be the right kind of age for me.' He paused, and the smile in his voice deepened. 'Say about thirty-three.'

Lizzy's heart had begun to thud, and she lay very still.

'A blonde would be good,' Tye went on softly. 'Yes, I think definitely a blonde, with a warm, lush body and legs that go on for ever.' Reaching out, he took hold of Lizzy's wrist and pulled her arm remorselessly away from her face, so that she was left staring up him, dry-mouthed and dark-eyed with temptation.

'I want a nice girl for a change.' His voice was very low. 'A nice girl and a hard worker.'

He was leaning over her now, smiling, blotting out the sun. Keeping hold of her wrist, he lifted her hand to his mouth and looked at the jagged line where the barbed wire had torn her skin. It was still red and raw-looking, but the bleeding had stopped.

'The sort of girl who mends fences and has the scars to prove it,' he said, kissing it before letting his lips drift teasingly to her wrist and on, down to the inside of her elbow, over her shoulder to linger along her collarbone and press slow, seductive kisses against her throat.

'Do you know anyone like that, Lizzy?' he asked, smiling into her skin.

Lizzy made an inarticulate noise, somewhere between a gasp and a moan, and turned her head in a despairing attempt to hide the treacherous response of her body that was yearning and quivering beneath the delicious on-slaught of his lips.

'No?' said Tye provocatively as they explored the line of her jaw. 'I do. I know someone just like that.' Dropping tiny, enticing kisses on the end of her nose, over her cheeks, in her hair, he whispered, 'Someone with blue, blue eyes; someone who looks like she smiles when she's asleep; someone...' his lips drifted downwards '...with a mouth just made for kissing.'

Lizzy was lost. There was no point in struggling, she told herself hazily as she gave herself up to the intoxicating pleasure of being able to wind her arms round Tye's neck and kiss him back. What could be wrong about something that felt this good? His mouth exploring hers, the taste of his tongue, his body pressing her down onto the warm rock... It felt so right that Lizzy couldn't believe she had resisted it for so long.

Tye's hands were moving over her in urgent possession, sliding insistently along her thigh, sweeping over the contours of her hip, curving around her breast. Lizzy arched beneath him, her own hands running feverishly over his back and shoulders as if she couldn't feel enough of him. His body was taut and unyielding, like steel beneath his warm, sleek skin, and she clung breathlessly to him as his mouth left hers to nuzzle her ear.

'Marry me, Lizzy,' he murmured, his voice ragged and uneven. 'We could be so good together. You know we could.'

They could... Lizzy could feel the dark undertow of desire, urging her to agree. Tye was right; it would be oh, so good.

Tye was sliding the strap of her swimsuit down and kissing her shoulder as he went. 'Say you'll marry me,' he whispered. 'Say yes. It might not be your dream, but this is enough, isn't it?'

Lizzy closed her eyes, trying to block out the clamour of her body that craved his touch, that didn't want him to stop. It would be so easy to say yes. If she said yes, he would peel the wet swimsuit off and make love to her. They were utterly alone. No one would find them out here, no one would know. They could make love until the sun went down, and then go back to the homestead and make love some more.

Say yes, her body urged.

If she said yes, she would be able to stay at Barra. She could be with Tye every day, every night. Wouldn't that be enough?

'Say yes,' said Tye again, lips warm and persuasive at her breast.

His mother had said yes. A chill crept into Lizzy's heart. Helen Gibson had mistaken sexual chemistry for love and paid the price. Did she really want to do the same? Tye might satisfy her physically, but they couldn't spend their whole time in bed. They wanted different things. He wanted Barra and she wanted love.

Tye was tugging down her other strap. 'I'll give you everything,' he said, as if he could read her mind. 'You don't need love as well.'

'I do,' said Lizzy brokenly. 'I do. That's just what I need.'

'What about this?' he asked, kissing her throat, her shoulder. 'You want me, Lizzy. I can feel it when I touch you, when I kiss you. Doesn't that mean anything?'

'It's not enough,' she said with difficulty, and he lifted his head to look down into her anguished blue eyes.

'You won't marry me?' he said, as if he couldn't believe what she was saying.

She shook her head. 'No,' she whispered, knowing that he wouldn't ask again.

'I see.' Tye's face hardened and he rolled abruptly away from her.

Lizzy sat up, miserably pulling her straps back into position. 'I'm sorry, Tye, I just—'

'Forget it,' he said. 'It would have been convenient, that's all.'

Convenient, she thought bitterly. She could see that it would have been convenient for him. A handy wife, already on the spot, ready to be presented to the executors of his father's will. A quick trip to get married with the minimum of fuss and Barra would be finally his. He could get back to his precious property and file her away and forget about her. Oh, yes, it would have been very convenient for Tye if she'd said yes.

Tye picked up a stone and threw it into the waterhole, where it disappeared with a plop that echoed in the strained silence.

'Looks as if I'd better go to that rodeo after all,' he said, and Lizzy's heart cracked to hear the hard note back in his voice.

'I'll go with you,' she promised. 'I won't marry you, but that doesn't mean I won't help you.'

'Big of you,' he said unpleasantly. 'Nothing whatsoever to do with the fat salary you're hoping to earn, I'm sure.'

'No,' said Lizzy, clasping her hands around her knees to stop them shaking. 'I'll do it because I know how much Barra means to you now. You still need a wife, and I can help you find one.'

'Lizzy?'

Lizzy's heart sank as she recognised her mother's voice. She should have called her parents to let them know that she would be here, but somehow the thought of all the explanations had seemed too much, and then she had been too content mending fences to want to tell anyone where she was or what she was doing.

'Hello, Mum.' She turned to kiss her mother dutifully.

'We thought you were in Perth!'

Tye turned as well, and her mother's expression of

astonishment turned to one of ludicrous dismay. 'Mrs Walker,' he greeted her coolly, and his keen gaze flickered between the two of them. 'You'll want to talk to your mother on your own,' he said to Lizzy, and walked away before she had a chance to object.

Lizzy looked after him with a mixture of frustration and relief. She wished that she had never remembered this wretched rodeo.

If she hadn't mentioned it they could have been out in the paddocks, still working together in the space and the light. If she had kept her mouth shut Tye wouldn't have asked her to marry him, she wouldn't have had to refuse. He wouldn't have kissed her, and they wouldn't have spent the evening in a silence jangling with tension.

Lizzy had done her best to pretend that nothing had happened and to carry on as normal, but Tye had refused to respond to her attempts to make conversation, and in the end she'd given up. How could she be normal anyway, when the memory of his kiss was still strumming in her blood and tingling over her skin?

She hated seeing the shuttered look that had returned to his eyes. She had hoped that he might relax once he got to the rodeo, but he had only stood grim-faced at her side as she'd introduced him round with feverish gaiety. He was obviously hating every moment, and had barely responded to her attempts to include him in the conversation.

This isn't what he's really like, Lizzy wanted to cry, but she didn't think that anyone would believe her.

They didn't know the Tye she knew. They hadn't seen him out under the Barra sky, banging a fence post into the ground, squinting at the horizon, smiling at her from under his hat.

Kissing her by the waterhole.

Don't think about it, Lizzy told herself desperately, and forced her mind back to the rodeo and the suspicious looks the others were giving Tye. They saw only a cold-eyed stranger with a hard mouth, and although no one had actually snubbed him yet, it had been made very clear that he would not have been welcome without her.

Lizzy had refused to admit defeat. She had pinned a bright smile to her face and dragged Tye from group to group, chatting vivaciously for everyone, and now she was exhausted with the effort of willing him to at least smile.

He would never find a wife looking like that, she thought in despair. He had to like *someone*. Lizzy had spent the night telling herself to forget the way he had kissed her. She might hate the idea of the callous, cold-blooded marriage Tye intended, but she had promised to help him and that was what she was going to do. She couldn't bear the thought of him having to leave Barra now, no matter what it cost.

'Lizzy, what are you doing here with that man?' demanded her mother as Tye walked off without a backward glance.

'His name is Tye Gibson,' said Lizzy frostily, 'and I'm his social secretary.'

That was what she had been telling everyone, although the more she said it, the less convincing it sounded. Few men looked less likely to need a social secretary than Tye Gibson!

'Social secretary?' Her mother sounded deeply suspicious. 'What kind of a job is that?'

'A well-paid one,' said Lizzy, trying to see where Tye had gone. 'Relax, Ma! It's just a job. You should be pleased for me.'

Her mother refused to be reassured. 'I don't like the

idea of you working for Tye Gibson,' she grumbled. 'Look at the way he treated Veronica Barenski! He threw her out of the house she'd been living in for ten years, and after all she'd done for his father!'

'He didn't throw her out.' Lizzy was surprised at how angry she felt. 'Veronica didn't want to stay.'

'That's not what Veronica says—or the Barra station hands. They wouldn't have anything to do with him, and from what I've heard I don't blame them!'

'That's their loss,' said Lizzy tightly. 'Honestly, you should listen to yourself, Mum! You go on about how big and hostile the city is, and how I should come home because everyone's so friendly, but I haven't seen anybody being very friendly to Tye. Nobody's even given him a chance!'

She was appalled to hear a distinct tremor in her voice, and forced herself to take a steadying breath. She didn't want her mother wondering why she was getting so upset on Tye's behalf. She didn't even want to wonder about it herself.

'Tye isn't nearly as black as he's been painted,' she said more calmly. 'I wouldn't be working for him if he was, would I? There are two sides to every story, so you can tell that to anyone who tries to tell you how badly he's treated Veronica and those men!'

Craning her neck, she spotted Tye at last in the distance. He was facing a group of young men who had been sitting on the rails around the makeshift ring, waiting to try their turn riding a wild bull or lassoing a calf. Lizzy couldn't hear what they were saying, but the body language was hostile and it was obvious that trouble was brewing.

'Look, Mum, I've got to go,' she said hurriedly. 'I'll give you a call soon.'

As quickly as she could without running, Lizzy walked over to where the men were squaring up to each other, apparently oblivious to the circle of spectators that was gathering around them.

'What's happening?' she asked one of them in a low voice.

'Seems like Gibson there asked those fellas why they wouldn't work at Barra any more,' he answered laconically.

'Oh, dear.' Lizzy pushed her way to the front of the circle. It was obvious that the station hands had been drinking. They were jeering and gesturing belligerently at Tye, whose face was a mask. There was something contemptuous about the way he stood there, and Lizzy could see that his aloofness was a provocation in itself as the stockmen tried to goad him into reacting.

'You don't think we're going to work for some pretty city boy, do you?' one of them sneered. 'You've been away too long, Tye Gibson, and you don't understand how things work here any more. You're too soft to survive in the outback.'

'Yeah,' another taunted. 'We've heard all about your fancy chefs and your private pilots. You've got someone to do everything, but...' He muttered a coarse aside to his fellows, who burst out laughing. 'How are you going to get your chauffeur on a horse?'

'I don't need a chauffeur. I can ride any horse here.' There was a white look about Tye's mouth, but his voice was perfectly level.

'Oh, yeah?' the other man scoffed. 'Want to prove that?'

'You don't need to prove anything,' said Lizzy quickly, moving to Tye's side and taking his arm, but he shook her off without even looking at her.

'You pick a horse and I'll ride it.'

The ringleader grinned unpleasantly and turned to a corral behind them, where a vicious-looking black stallion that was being kept with the others for the bucking bronco competition was running wildly round the pen. 'Think you can ride that one, Mr Big?' he asked, and they all sniggered.

'Yes.'

Tye's quiet, cold voice cut through the air, and there was a rustle among the spectators as the mood changed.

'This has gone far enough,' Lizzy began, but Tye simply moved her aside.

'You get that horse in the ring, and I'll ride it,' he told the men.

'Don't be so stupid,' she said in a fierce undertone as they ran to corner the horse and manoeuvre it into the race, where Tye would be able to drop onto its back. 'That's a dangerous animal! You'll get hurt! They're just trying to humiliate you.'

'They're not going to succeed,' said Tye, and his eyes were as cold as ice.

'Tye—' She tried to catch hold of his arm, but he brushed her off.

'Keep out of this, Lizzy,' he snarled.

Leaving her staring after him in frustration, he headed purposefully towards the race. It took ten men to force the stallion into the narrow pen, and the sound of its hooves kicking savagely against the boards made her blood run cold. She wanted to run away and hide, but she had to know what was happening, so she stood at the edge of the ring and watched helplessly as Tye leapt onto the horse's back, took hold of its mane and the gate was opened.

The stallion erupted into the ring, bucking furiously,

snorting and shaking its head. Its hooves flashed viciously as it reared and kicked, and Lizzy's hands crept unconsciously to her throat. The crowd had fallen silent, and even those who had drifted over for the bucking bronco competition and hadn't heard the altercation sensed that this was no ordinary, light-hearted contest.

Lizzy was terrified. She had never seen a horse as savage as this one. It seemed to fill the ring, its eyes rolling, hooves lashing, foaming with fury and frustration. If Tye fell, he wouldn't stand a chance under the maddened creature. It would trample him to death. One blow from those hooves would be enough.

Rigid with fear, Lizzy waited every second for Tye to crash to the ground. There was no way he could stay on, she thought desperately, dreading the moment when he would be thrown, but unable to look away.

She never knew how long she stood there, watching as he clung to the back of that mean horse, riding its punishing bucks, dominating the animal by the sheer force of his will, but after what seemed like a lifetime the horse, incredibly, began to tire. One moment it seemed to Lizzy that it was lashing out furiously, and the next it was slowing in defeat, until it was walking round the ring, still sweating and snorting, its flanks heaving, but the fight gone out of it.

There was utter silence round the ring. Lizzy didn't wait to see how the crowd would react. Having prayed more desperately than she had ever prayed in her life for Tye not to fall, she was paradoxically furious the moment she was sure that he wasn't hurt. Blind with sheer, unreasoning rage, she pushed her way back out of the crowd, not caring where she went so long as it was as far away from Tye as possible.

She was so angry that she didn't even notice the man

heading towards her until she had literally bumped into him.

'Whoah! Where are you off to in such a hurry?' he asked in amusement.

'Oh…Gray!' The red mist cleared slightly as she recognised one of her oldest friends. 'I'm sorry, I just… Why are men so *stupid*?' she burst out, unable to finish her sentence.

Wisely, Gray didn't try to answer this. He led her to a quiet spot in the shade, sat her down and brought her a beer instead. 'Now, tell me what the matter is,' he said.

He listened without comment as Lizzy raged about the stupid, reckless irresponsibility of brainless, mindless, moronic men who would put their lives at risk rather than lose face, and gradually his restful presence had its effect. Having got it all off her chest, Lizzy suddenly found that she had talked herself out and stopped.

She looked at Gray, who was calmly waiting for her to carry on, and she laughed a little shakily. 'Thanks, Gray. I needed that.' She hugged him gratefully. 'Now, I'm not going to rant and rave any more. I want to hear about you instead. How's Clare, and the baby? Is everything OK?'

Gray gave her a rather searching look, but he let her change the subject, and by the time he had told her about his wife, and the baby they were expecting, Lizzy was feeling much calmer.

They were still sitting there talking when Tye found them some time later. 'What are you doing hiding over here?' he said irritably to Lizzy, and turned a basilisk stare on Gray, who was not easily intimidated and merely looked back at him without expression.

'I'm not hiding,' Lizzy snapped, ruffling up immediately. The calming effect of Gray's presence counted for nothing when a few words from Tye were enough to set her on edge again. 'I just didn't feel like watching any more stupid stunts!'

'It wasn't a stunt,' said Tye coldly. 'It was the only way I was ever going to get any stockmen to work for me.'

'I've heard that advertising a job sometimes works!'

He ignored her sarcasm. 'Advertising isn't any good with men like these. I had to get their respect first.'

'Oh, *respect*! Of course, that's a very good idea, to risk your life just to impress a few creeps who wouldn't know respect from a poke in the eye with a sharp stick!'

'It worked, didn't it? I've got six men ready and willing to start next week.'

For some reason this news only made Lizzy crosser. 'Oh, well, that's all right then!' she said scornfully. 'What's a little dicing with death when you can get your fences mended sooner?'

Tye's mouth tightened. 'What's biting you?'

'Nothing,' said Lizzy, who wasn't even sure herself why she was so upset. 'I just thought that it was a stupid risk to take!'

Gray smiled slightly as he got to his feet. 'I'd give up if I were you,' he said to Tye. 'She'll never understand.' He turned back to Lizzy. 'I'd better go. Clare will be waiting for me, and I said I wouldn't be long.'

'Give her my love.' Lizzy stood up too and gave him a big hug. 'Thanks for listening, Gray.'

'Any time.' Gray returned her hug, and nodded pleasantly to Tye. 'See you both at the races,' he said, and walked off with his easy, unhurried stride.

Lizzy looked after him affectionately and Tye's eyes narrowed. 'Who was that?' he demanded in a glacial voice.

'Gray Henderson. If you hadn't been looking so grim I would have introduced you, but I didn't see why I should give you the chance to be rude to him. He's one of my oldest friends.'

'I gathered that,' said Tye, his mouth snapping like a trap. 'I didn't realise that I was paying you to spend the afternoon cosying up to *old friends*, though! You were supposed to have been working.'

'I was, as a matter of fact,' said Lizzy, her manner as frosty as his. 'The Hendersons always have a party after the races; everybody goes. Thanks to my "cosying up", as you call it, you're invited as well.'

Tye grunted. 'How did you manage that?'

'We don't all have to throw ourselves on the backs of wild stallions to get something done,' she said waspishly. 'I took the easy option and simply asked him to invite you.'

'Didn't he want to know why?'

'Gray's not like that. He's not nosy or suspicious about people's motives. He's a decent man.' Lizzy tried to think of a way to describe Gray in the kind of words that Tye would understand, but the two men were so different she couldn't imagine a way to bridge the gulf between them. 'He's wonderful,' was all she said in the end.

Tye's expression hardened. *'He's wonderful!'* he mimicked nastily. 'Just your type! Why don't you line him up as Mr Right?' he sneered, and Lizzy's eyes flashed dangerously.

'I thought he was once,' she said, goaded into betraying something she would have preferred not to have told Tye. 'We were engaged when we were younger.'

'Engaged?' The black brows snapped together. 'I thought it was Stephen you were engaged to?'

'That was another time.'

'Australia seems to be littered with your ex-fiancés!' His lip curled. 'Are there any more I should know about?'

Lizzy put up her chin. 'No—not that it's any of your business!'

'I'm beginning to wonder if you're the best person to find me wife,' Tye drawled. 'You obviously know a lot about the business of getting engaged, but you don't have a good track record at getting to the altar, do you? What did Gray Henderson do wrong?'

'He didn't do anything wrong!' She flushed angrily. She should never have told Tye about her other engagement! 'We were both very young, and we both realised that we weren't right for each other before it was too late. We agreed to be friends instead, and that's what we are. Very good friends.'

'Someone else who didn't live up to your exacting standards of romance!' he commented sardonically. 'There are a lot of us around, aren't there?'

'I wouldn't say that.' Lizzy cast him a look of dislike. 'Gray's the least romantic of men, but he's found exactly what I'm looking for. He's got a wife he adores, and who adores him, and if you saw them together maybe you'd begin to understand what love is really all about!'

'I don't need to understand,' said Tye harshly as he turned away. 'I just need a wife.'

Two of the men Tye had hired had come to the rodeo looking for work, and opted to go straight to Barra that night while they had a chance of a lift. Neither was a great conversationalist, but Lizzy was glad of their company in the back seat of the big four-wheel drive.

Tye was in filthy mood. Out of the corner of her eye she could see his glowering profile. His black brows were drawn together over the bridge of his nose and his lips were clamped tightly together, while a tell-tale muscle worked in his jaw.

What did *he* have to be so angry about? Lizzy wondered. He wasn't the one who had spent all day trying to make friends for him, and getting absolutely no thanks for it! He was rude and unreasonable and pig-headed, and it would have served him right if he *had* fallen off that stupid horse!

Lizzy had hated every moment of the rodeo, but at least it had taught her one thing, she reassured herself. She had made absolutely the right decision in not marrying Tye.

Tye was up early the next morning and went out with the new station hands. Lizzy, pointedly not included in his plans, was left to drift disconsolately around the homestead. She might have decided that he was a monumental pain, but it was annoying to discover that she still missed him when he wasn't there.

She didn't know what to do with herself now. Her mind kept drifting off to the paddocks where the men would be working, wondering if they had finished that section of fence, or done anything about the drinking trough.

Wondering if Tye was missing her, too.

What's wrong with me? Lizzy asked her glum reflection. I should be fantasising about shoe shops or cappuccinos, not about mending fences!

Eventually she remembered the party she had been going to organise. Tye might not have shown much enthusiasm for the idea, and judging by his attitude yesterday a party was the last thing he wanted, but she might as well do something. Her only alternative was to spend the day trying not to think about the waterhole and how good it had felt to kiss him. And Lizzy was already tired of trying—and failing—to do that.

No, organising a big party was a much better idea. Tye's birthday was less than six weeks away, and time was running out. She could get on with things and keep her mind occupied at the same time. Digging out her personal organiser, Lizzy settled down behind the desk in his office, where the only phone was installed. She would start by making some calls.

CHAPTER NINE

TYE'S office was intimidatingly efficient. Lizzy eyed the array of all the latest electronic wizardry uneasily as she picked up the phone. It wasn't that she distrusted technology, she had her own PC at home and was an enthusiastic e-mailer, but there was something so impersonal about this room that she felt distinctly uncomfortable.

There were no notes stuck around the computer screen, no cartoons or postcards pinned to the wall. In fact, there was no clutter at all, nothing that might give a clue to Tye's personality. It was hard to believe that anyone could work here, let alone the kind of man who would take you swimming in a hidden waterhole and kiss you on the warm rock.

Oh, God! She wasn't supposed to be thinking about that kiss. Lizzy caught herself up guiltily. She had made her decision—the right decision—and that was the end of the matter. Straightening her shoulders, she punched out the first number.

She was calculating the cost of hiring a band and flying them in for the day when Tye appeared without warning in the doorway.

'What are you doing in here?' he demanded.

Lizzy started, her heart jerking wildly at the unexpected sight of him. 'Doing my job,' she said, irritated as much by her own hopeless reaction as by the set expression on Tye's face.

'We agreed to have a party here the weekend after the races, if you remember. That's only three weeks away.

If I don't get something arranged soon, it will be too late. I presume you do still want a party?' she added when Tye only looked down his nose.

'You might as well go ahead,' he grunted. 'I just hope it's a better idea than your last one! The rodeo was a complete waste of time!'

'Whose fault was that?' retorted Lizzy crossly. 'It would have been fine if you'd made the slightest effort! I introduced you to loads of suitable girls!'

'I wouldn't have called any of them suitable,' said Tye, throwing himself into the black leather chair and swivelling morosely.

'They were all single, and born and bred in the outback,' she pointed out. 'There must have been one you liked?'

Tye's jaw set stubbornly. 'There wasn't.'

'What about Melissa Martin?'

'Especially not her.'

Lizzy couldn't help feeling secretly pleased. She didn't like Melissa either.

'OK, what about Emma Phillips?'

'Did you see her teeth?'

Lizzy sighed. 'You're very fussy all of sudden! I thought you didn't care what your wife looked like as long as you got Barra?'

'If I'm going to spend the rest of my life with her, I might as well find her attractive,' said Tye, sounding defensive. Restlessly, he got to his feet and prowled over to the fax machine to check if anything of interest had come in.

Hearing a sigh from behind the desk, he rounded on Lizzy. 'I know you're thinking of your bonus,' he said nastily, 'and there's no need to panic! I'll find someone, and I'll marry her before June. That's something you can bet on!'

She ought to be pleased, Lizzy thought dully. Unable to meet his eyes, she doodled around the figures she had scribbled into her notebook. 'What are you doing here, anyway?' she asked tiredly. 'I thought you would be finishing that fence.'

'I've left the men doing that.' Deprived of the angry reaction he had expected, Tye abandoned the fax and paced over to switch on the computer instead. 'I came back to ring Sydney,' he admitted grudgingly. 'We've got a problem.'

'What sort of problem?'

'Apparently there was a bit of a showdown at breakfast this morning. The station hands weren't impressed with the fancy food they were given last night, and they insisted on having steak and eggs for breakfast. The chef is now in revolt and demanding to go back to Sydney straight away, as are the other staff.'

'I told you they wouldn't last long,' Lizzy was unable to resist pointing out. 'What are you going to do now?'

'Get my assistant to find replacements as soon as possible.'

'I wouldn't bother,' she said frankly. 'All you need is a cook, and you'd be much better off finding someone local who knows better than to serve up anything except roast beef and meatloaf.'

Tye frowned. 'How do you suggest I do that?'

'I'll ask around,' offered Lizzy, even though part of her was wondering why on earth she should put herself out for Tye when he was being so unpleasant. 'In the meantime, I may as well do the cooking myself.'

He looked at her quickly, his expression lightening. 'Would you really?'

For some reason, Lizzy couldn't quite meet his eyes. 'It'll give me something to do,' she said, carefully filling in her doodles.

'I'm not cooking two lots of meals,' she warned him when he tried to thank her. 'And I'm certainly not running up and down to the dining room! You can all come and eat in the kitchen together. It will give you a chance to get to know the station hands properly, anyway.'

So Lizzy took charge of the kitchen. She was glad to be busy, but she missed being out on the land. She missed driving out at dawn and drinking billy tea in the shade.

She missed Tye.

As the days passed, the terrible tension between them settled into a careful politeness. She saw him every day, of course, but hardly ever on his own. The four other men he had hired at the rodeo arrived at the end of the week, and they all ate together. Tye spent the day outside, and after the evening meal he would closet himself with his computer in his office.

Nothing was the same any more, Lizzy thought miserably. There were no more cold beers on the verandah, no more plans over the dining table. It was only by asking the station hands that she even knew what they were doing.

Eventually she managed to track down a cook, who let herself be lured to Barra in exchange for generous wages that were still only a fraction of what Tye had been paying the Sydney staff. Once Karen had arrived Lizzy had nothing to do again but carry on with the arrangements for the party.

She threw herself into the organisation, telling herself that it was the kind of job she loved to do, and much more suited to her talents than mending fences. It was good experience too.

She should be thinking about the future, Lizzy reasoned, not the days when she and Tye had been alone. There was no point in wishing that Tye would involve her more. He would be forty soon. He would find himself a wife, just as he had sworn to do, and she would have no reason to stay. She might as well get used to not being with him now.

The race course at Mathison was little more than a dusty track between single rails. There was a beer tent, and a bookie whose preparations hadn't involved more than propping a blackboard on which he had chalked the odds for the first race on a chair in the shade. Horses stood patiently in the enclosure, flicking their tails against the flies, but until the racing started most people were more interested in meeting friends than eyeing up likely winners.

There had been a grim determination about Tye as he drove Lizzy from Barra. 'I don't want to waste any more time,' he'd told her. 'I've got to meet someone today, or it will be too late.'

'Fine,' Lizzy had said bleakly.

It was the first time they had been alone for two weeks. The station hands were planning to spend the evening in the pub and Karen had opted to go with them. Tye had given them permission to stay the night in Mathison and return to Barra the next day. 'It's just you and me,' he had said to Lizzy when she'd gone out to join him in the car.

She should have been enjoying herself, Lizzy thought as she introduced Tye to yet another single woman. Normally she loved the races, which were one of the social occasions of the year, and she couldn't even complain that Tye was not making an effort this time.

Attitudes towards him seemed to have softened considerably since the rodeo. It might have been the way he had mastered the stallion, or the wary respect in which the men now working at Barra held him, or maybe even her own efforts in the general store at Mathison to persuade people that he was not the monster his father had made him out to be.

Whatever the reason, Tye was greeted, if not with the same warmth as Lizzy, then at least without outright hostility this time, and he was following up on his advantage. Women who had pursed their lips at the rodeo, or boasted in the store that they weren't impressed by his money and would have nothing to do with him, were now simpering and smirking like schoolgirls. Tye was laying on the charm, and it was working.

Just as it had done with her.

She had been so sure that she was only one who understood him, Lizzy thought with an edge of bitterness. Tye had made her feel special. Why had she never noticed before how skilful he was at manipulating conversation?

She watched him as if from a great distance. It was like watching a big cat cut its prey out of the herd. Tye was utterly focused on what he was doing. Somehow he managed to isolate a single woman in conversation until he had found out what he wanted to know, and then he moved on, without anyone in the group being aware of what he had done. He would nod farewell and leave them to agree that rumour had lied and he wasn't nearly as bad as he had been painted.

Lizzy felt completely redundant, but Tye insisted on her staying close by his side. It was almost as if he wanted to prove to her how little he needed her. Few women were proof against his smile when he chose to use it, and they were soon falling over themselves to talk to him. Every time Lizzy saw his head bend intimately down, every time his smile flashed, it was like a knife turning in her heart. She had thought he only smiled like that for her.

Now he was nose to nose with the stock agent's pretty daughter, Julie, who had a heart-shaped face and big brown eyes and was plainly dazzled by Tye. Lizzy saw him touch Julie's elbow lightly, and a boiling tide of jealousy surged terrifyingly along her veins. She wanted to leap between them, to slap Tye's hand down, to push Julie away from him, to shout at them both to stop smiling and looking and touching like that.

She might even have started forward, for at that moment Tye turned his head, as if to check her reaction. He looked full into her eyes, and then deliberately away, and Lizzy's heart plummeted sickeningly as the ground dropped away beneath her feet.

Oh, no! she prayed. No, no, *no*.

Around her, people were talking and laughing, but Lizzy couldn't hear anything. Their lips moved soundlessly, and behind them the horses on the track glided silently past, their hooves making no noise as they raced towards the finishing line. Lizzy was separated from it all by an invisible, impenetrable barrier that cut her off from the world and left her alone with the dull recognition of how much she loved him.

Love isn't meant to be like this, she wanted to cry. Her destiny was supposed to burst gloriously into her life, instant and unmistakable, not creep up on her when she least wanted it.

She didn't want to be in love with Tye! She wanted

someone who would recognise her as his soul mate, someone who would know as soon as he looked at her that they had to be together. She wanted it to be perfect.

And instead it was Tye. Tye, who didn't believe in love. Tye, who didn't need anyone. Tye, who was standing beside her, cold-bloodedly intent on marriage with anyone who would fall for his calculating charm. The way she had done.

Lizzy felt nauseous, slightly giddy. People were beginning to look at her in concern, and she managed to muster a smile, but it was a relief when Tye took her arm and moved them away.

He looked down at her, frowning. 'What's the matter with you?' he demanded. 'You look like you've seen a ghost!'

'I'm perfectly all right.' Lizzy pulled her arm away, terrified that he would be able to see how she loved him. She didn't think that she could bear that.

Tye's eyes narrowed, but to her relief he didn't pursue it. 'Things are looking up,' he said instead. 'I think Julie might make a good Mrs Gibson, don't you?'

'No,' she said flatly. 'She's too young for you.'

'She's very pretty,' he mused.

Lizzy wondered if he could hear heart cracking. Her throat felt tight and it was an effort to speak. 'I thought you didn't believe in big age gaps?' she managed, remembering how he had murmured in her ear as they lay by the waterhole, how his hand had slid over her thigh.

'Hmm, perhaps you're right,' Tye acknowledged. 'We'd better look for someone a bit older.'

His cool gaze swept the crowd. 'Who's that woman over there?' he asked, nodding his head towards a redhead studying the odds on the bookie's blackboard.

Was he deliberately trying to hurt her? 'Aileen Rogers,' said Lizzy dully.

'Is she single?'

'Divorced.'

'Excellent,' said Tye. 'There was nothing in the will about my wife not being married before. A divorcee would be ideal. She's certainly unlikely to have as many romantic illusions about marriage as some people,' he added pointedly.

Lizzy didn't reply.

'She's very attractive, too.' He looked down at Lizzy with a taunting gleam in his eyes. 'Don't you agree?'

'If you like red hair,' said Lizzy through stiff lips.

'I'm not fussy.' He renewed his study of Aileen. 'I don't think you'd be able to say that *she* was too young. Have you got any other objections?'

Lizzy's hands were curled into fists, the nails digging into her palms. 'It's not up to me,' she pointed out through gritted teeth, convinced that he was deliberately punishing her. 'You're the one that's thinking about marrying her.'

'I think I'd better meet her before I go that far,' said Tye. 'Why don't you introduce us?'

Lizzy had suddenly had enough. 'Introduce yourself,' she said, her voice cracking dangerously. 'I'm going to get a drink.'

Unable to face the crowd in the beer tent, she went to lean on the enclosure fence and look at the waiting horses instead. Her hat was like a tight band around her head and she took it off, running her fingers through her hair as the pressure eased. A roar went up behind her as a race ended, but Lizzy didn't turn round. She was staring at the horses but she was seeing the waterhole at

Barra Creek, and Tye, leaning above her, bending to kiss her throat.

Marry me, he had said.

And she had said no.

It had been her own choice. It had been the right choice. She couldn't complain now that he was looking for a wife elsewhere, but it didn't stop the turmoil raging in her heart when she imagined Tye smiling down at Aileen Rogers, kissing her, asking *her* to marry him instead, because when it came down to it any woman would do.

Absorbed in her miserable thoughts, Lizzy wasn't aware of Gray's approach until he leant on the fence beside her. 'Is everything OK, Lizzy?' he asked. 'It's not like you to hang around the edges. You're usually the life and soul of a party!'

Lizzy took a breath and willed her trembling mouth to steady. 'Oh, I'm just…'

Just trying not to cry.

Just wondering if she had thrown away her only chance at happiness.

Just wishing things could be different.

'I'm just having a day off,' she said lamely.

Gray glanced at her averted profile. Her mouth was pressed into a fiercely straight line. 'Is it Tye?' he asked gently.

The mouth wavered and then steadied with an obvious effort of will. 'Sort of,' she muttered.

Gray was a very restful friend. He didn't probe or exclaim or insist that she went into details. He simply put his arm round her and offered her the calm comfort of his presence. Lizzy leant gratefully against him, unable to talk even if she had wanted to, and fought down the tight knot of tears in her throat.

After a few minutes she let out a long, wavering sigh, swallowed hard, and straightened. 'Clare is a very, very lucky girl,' she told Gray.

He smiled and flicked her gently on the cheek. 'You let me know if you ever want me to punch Tye Gibson on the nose,' he said, and Lizzy managed a shaky laugh.

'I might take you up on that!'

'Are you still coming to the barbecue at Bushman's Creek?'

'Yes, of course,' she said, although all she wanted was to curl up somewhere on her own and cry.

'I'll see you later, then.'

Left alone once more, Lizzy took a few deep breaths before squaring her shoulders. She couldn't cry, and she couldn't stay here either. She was going to have to face Tye some time, so it might as well be now.

Reluctantly she turned, to find herself looking straight into glacial grey eyes, and her heart jerked agonisingly. 'I was just coming to look for you,' she faltered.

'Oh, so you remembered me!' His words were a series of rat traps snapping shut. 'I guess I should feel flattered that you even gave me a thought. I'm only the guy who's paying you a big, fat salary, and you've obviously got much more important things to do, like snuggling up to your very good friend Gray Henderson!'

So this was it, Lizzy thought wearily. She couldn't even convince herself that she had merely been swept off her feet by superficial charm and glamour. She had fallen in love with a bad-tempered, pig-headed man, and she still loved him even when he was being obnoxious, like now.

Welcome to true love. It wasn't what she had thought it would be, that was for sure.

There was little point in arguing with him when he

was in this mood. 'What do you want?' she asked drearily.

'You said you were going to get a drink,' Tye reminded her accusingly. 'I looked for you in the beer tent, but you weren't there.'

'I changed my mind.'

'You *are* supposed to be my social secretary.' Tye scowled. 'Not that anyone would guess it from the way you're skulking over here!'

Lizzy pushed her hair wearily back from her face. 'You seemed to be getting on fine without me. I would just have cramped your style with Aileen Rogers.' She glanced at him. 'You didn't talk to her for very long.'

Tye's eyes flickered. 'Long enough,' he said brusquely. 'I invited her to the party.'

'Is she going to come?'

'She can't wait.'

Well, that figured. Aileen Rogers was no fool, and if she had sensed Tye's interest she would waste no time in capitalising on it. Aileen had never been one for coyly hanging back, Lizzy remembered with a tightening of the heart.

'It sounds as if you got on all right,' she made herself say.

Tye hesitated imperceptibly. 'She seems ideal.'

'Good.' There was a cold stone inside her, getting heavier and heavier by the second, its weight dragging her down until it was all Lizzy could do to keep upright.

Tye seemed bent on rubbing salt into the wound. 'You'd better make sure that she gets a proper invitation when you send the others out.'

'Sure.'

There was a pause. Lizzy could feel Tye's eyes boring into her, but she couldn't look at him. She put her hat on, hoping that the broad brim would hide her expression, but it didn't seem to do much good.

'You look tired,' said Tye roughly, almost as if the words had been forced out of him against his will.

'I've got a bit of a headache, that's all.'

'We might as well go, in that case.'

'But...don't you want to meet anyone else?'

'No.' His voice was abrupt.

He must be sure that Aileen was just the kind of woman he was looking for, thought Lizzy miserably.

'I told Gray that we'd go to the barbecue at Bushman's Creek,' she said.

'I'm sure you did,' said Tye with a snap. 'But I don't see why I should hang around just so that you can have another chance to cuddle up to Mr Perfect, with his perfect wife and his perfect marriage! I'm not sure his wife would think it was quite so perfect if she saw how he can't keep his hands off you!'

Lizzy shook her head. 'You don't understand,' she said.

'Oh, I understand all right!' he practically snarled. 'Come on, we're going back to Barra right now.'

Mathison had never seen a party like it. There were jugglers and magicians, face-painters and puppet shows to entertain the children. A team of cooks, flown in from Perth, stood behind vast barbecues laden with sizzling seafood and steaks, while tables in the specially erected marquee groaned with a mouthwatering array of salads and desserts.

It was a perfect day. A few cirrus clouds streaked the blue sky, and a light breeze kept the temperature down. A band played in the background, the drink flowed, and the guests drifted happily around. As Lizzy had predicted, almost everyone had overcome their scruples, and they were all making the most of the opportunity to see Barra and enjoy a taste of Tye Gibson's fabled wealth.

Lizzy herself was shattered after a week of frantically busy days and sleepless nights. In a way she had been grateful for the fact that there had been so much to do to get ready for the party that she had had little time to think, but the nights had been much harder.

Night after night, she had lain awake, wondering how it could have taken her so long to realise that she had fallen in love with Tye. Everything had been so much simpler when it had seemed no more than a physical attraction. Now she had to face up to spending the rest of her life without the one person who could make her feel complete.

Why did it have to be Tye? Why couldn't she have fallen in love with a kind, decent, *nice* man, who lived like her and thought like her and wanted the same things that she did? A man who would have loved her and needed her and made her feel safe.

Instead it was Tye, and there was nothing Lizzy could do about it. She had never dreamed that love could hurt so much physically. Her heart felt raw and bruised with every beat, her body ached, and she learnt to take quick, shallow breaths, as if steeling herself against some inner pain.

Sometimes she wondered why she didn't just give in. She could throw her pride to the wind and tell Tye that she had changed her mind. She could still marry him. At least she would be with him, temptation whispered. Wouldn't that be better than nothing? Tye might sneer at her motives, but he would still take her, Lizzy was sure of it. He might be putting all his efforts into wooing

Aileen now, but he hadn't asked her yet, and Lizzy was still convenient.

Convenient. The word always brought her up short. Could she really give up all her dreams for a man who would marry her just because it was convenient? It would be a betrayal of everything she believed in, Lizzy realised. It would cheapen her love and make it seem tawdry and tatty, something to be bargained away instead of treasured.

And how long would it last anyway, in the face of Tye's indifference? How long before it shrivelled up and turned to bitterness and resentment as his mother's had?

No, thought Lizzy, she deserved better than that.

It was a fabulous party. People kept telling her so, so she supposed it must be true, but she couldn't wait for it to be over. She stood on the front verandah, looking out over the laughing crowds and the waiters circulating with their bottles, and wished that they would all go home. She wished the band would shut up, and the entertainers would disappear, and the caterers would clear up and leave. But most of all she wished she could rewind time back to the waterhole, when she and Tye had been utterly alone and the only sound had been the whirring of the insects in the hot, still air.

Her jaw ached from the effort of smiling, and she was trembling inside with the strain of appearing her usual cheerful self when it felt as if her whole world was falling apart.

Ashamed of her own need to keep him in sight, Lizzy had managed to keep a surreptitious eye on Tye as he moved around the party greeting people, but in the last half-hour he had disappeared and she was getting ridiculously twitchy, wondering where he was, who he was with and what he was doing.

Not that it was hard to guess. Tye had rung Aileen twice since the races, and on Thursday he had actually ordered the jet up from Sydney to collect them in Mathison so that he could take her out to lunch in Darwin. Aileen, he had taken great pleasure in telling Lizzy, didn't waste her time on stupid sentimentality. She was like him—knew what she wanted and went all out to get it. In fact, Tye had concluded, they had a lot in common.

Sometimes Lizzy wondered if he were deliberately going out of his way to hurt her. In spite of finding a kindred spirit in Aileen, he had been in a vile mood all week, and had spent his whole time sniping at her, criticising the arrangements she had made for the party or ringing Aileen when he knew that she was in the office and would be able to overhear every word of his conversation.

Lizzy had gritted her teeth and reminded herself that she had wanted him to find a wife. Married, he would be able to stay at Barra, and she would go back to Perth with a lot of money. She ought to be glad that he had found someone as suitable as Aileen, not dreading the moment when they would announce their engagement.

What if he were asking Aileen to marry him right now? The party would be the perfect time for them both to slip away and agree their cold-blooded deal. Lizzy looked around for Tye in sudden panic, but she couldn't see him. She spotted her mother, rolling her eyes and gesticulating, talking to Gray and Clare. There was Jack, wiping ice cream from his baby daughter's face, and Ellie, watching the two of them with a smile. There was—

There was Tye!

Lizzy's gaze jerked to a halt as she caught sight of

his lean, familiar figure through the crowds. He was standing next to a woman, his dark head very close to hers, and even from a distance Lizzy could tell that it was Aileen. Her red hair was unmistakable.

Not wanting to watch, but unable to tear her eyes away, Lizzy saw Aileen stand on tiptoe and whisper in Tye's ear. He smiled and put a hand to her waist, drawing her away from the crowd, and jealousy clawed so savagely at Lizzy's heart that she had to clap a hand to her mouth to stifle the cry that rose to her lips.

Heedless of who might see her, she turned and ran through the house and down the back steps, stumbling onto the dappled shade of the creek until the music and the laughter was only a faint sound in the distance. She was panting when she stopped at last, and the bush seemed to be spinning around her, taunting her with its serenity and its silence.

Sick and giddy, Lizzy sank down onto a fallen tree. She couldn't remember getting here. All she remembered was Tye's smile, and Aileen leaning close to him, whispering in his ear. She pressed the heels of her hands against her eyes to block out the image, but it was no good. Her mind was like a video, endlessly stuck on 'pause', freezing them in that moment of intimacy, smiling, touching, turning away from the rest of the crowd.

Lizzy drew a shuddering breath and opened her eyes. It was very still, and as she sat the tranquillity and silence settled slowly around her, no longer mocking but insensibly comforting.

With sudden clarity she realised how badly she was behaving. It wasn't Tye's fault that she had fallen in love with him. He had been absolutely honest with her, and she couldn't complain now that he wasn't the person she wanted him to be. Tye was the way he was, and he wasn't going to change for her or for anyone else. She could take him or she could leave him, and it was her decision to leave.

She was lucky, Lizzy reminded herself. She lived in a wonderful city, where she had a home, friends, a career. It was time that she went back to them all. And perhaps one day she would meet someone else and discover that love didn't have to be like this. Perhaps then she would be able to look back at her feelings for Tye and marvel that she could have been so unhappy because of him.

Perhaps.

CHAPTER TEN

IT WAS dark before the last guests left. The band had packed up, the entertainers were relaxing with well-earned beers in the old cookhouse, the waiters were stacking the last tables, and Lizzy could escape to the back verandah and stop smiling at last. She was curled up in a cane chair, half hidden in a shadowy corner, when Tye found her.

'So there you are!' he said irritably. 'What are you doing sitting out here in the dark?'

'It's been a long day.' Lizzy was too tired to pretend any more. 'I thought I was entitled to some time to my-self.'

Tye ignored the hint. He seemed restless, pacing the verandah, leaning on the rail, straightening, pacing some more. A rectangle of yellow light angled across the dark-ness further down, illuminating his features momentarily before he turned back to the shadows, where Lizzy waited silently for him to get whatever it was he had to say off his chest.

Every time he came near her she wanted to put out her hand and make him stop, to persuade him to sit beside her in the dark and listen to the night. This would be the last chance she had to be alone with him, and she ought to make the most of it, but she didn't trust herself not to cry.

It felt as if there was a vice tightening cruelly around her heart, a savage hand around her throat. Lizzy didn't dare move or speak in case she fell apart. All she could do was sit there desperately hanging onto her control. She *mustn't* break down.

'I just wanted to thank you,' Tye said abruptly at last. He had stopped by the steps and in the darkness his expression was impossible to decipher. 'The party was a big success, and it was all due to you. I know how hard you worked to get everything organised.'

'I was just doing my job,' she said in a constricted voice.

There was the tiniest of pauses. 'Your job,' Tye echoed, so heavily that Lizzy could almost believe that he'd forgotten. He turned and leant on the verandah rail with his back to her. 'Yes, I guess it was.'

'I enjoyed doing it,' Lizzy went on, finding it easier now that he wasn't looking at her. 'And it's been good experience for me. I…' She took breath and forged on. 'I've decided to specialise in events management when I get back to Perth.'

'Perth?' Tye swung round. 'I thought you wanted to work for GCS in London?'

She *had* said that, Lizzy remembered. She thought about the day they had finished work in the yards, and how Tye had sat with his hands on the wheel of the ute. 'The job's yours,' he had told her, and she had had to pretend to be pleased.

'I've changed my mind,' she said, avoiding his eyes. 'I'd rather stay in Perth and set up my own business organising big parties, conferences, publicity launches… that kind of thing. I think I'd be quite good at it,' she added defiantly, as if Tye had pooh-poohed the whole idea. 'All I need is a bit of capital to get me going.'

There was a raw silence. 'I see,' said Tye after a moment. 'Well, don't worry, it won't be long and you can have your capital. That's what we agreed.'

'You're…you're getting married?'

'Yes.'

Lizzy dug her nails into her palms. 'To Aileen?'

'Yes.'

It was funny, Lizzy thought with an odd, detached part of her mind. She had been dreading this moment, and she had known that it would hurt, but she hadn't had any idea of just how agonising it would be. She clutched herself around the stomach, where the pain was worst, and refused to let herself break down. Her pride wasn't much comfort but it was all she had.

'Does she know why you're so keen to get married?' she asked in a voice that sounded thin and squeezed of air.

'Not yet.' Tye put his hands in his pockets and scowled. 'I haven't had a chance to explain the situation yet. I'll do it when I ask her to marry me.'

Lizzy's heart leapt, even though she knew it was futile. 'You haven't asked her yet?'

'No. I'm going to talk to her tomorrow.'

'She might not say yes.'

'She will,' said Tye. 'You don't get to run a billion-dollar business without being able to predict how people are going to react.'

'I said no,' Lizzy reminded him, lifting her head to look him straight in the eyes. 'You didn't predict that.'

They stared at each other through the shadows for a long, jangling moment, and then Tye looked away. 'Aileen won't,' he said flatly. 'She'll say yes all right, when she hears what's on offer.'

He was probably right, Lizzy thought dully as she

uncurled her legs and got stiffly to her feet. Aileen wasn't stupid.

So this was it, the end of the line. No point now in hoping that Tye would change and fall in love. No point in hoping that Aileen would turn down the chance of securing her future by marrying an attractive man and sharing his millions.

Only a fool would do that.

Only a fool like her.

'Well…congratulations,' she said, unable to keep the desolation from her voice.

'You don't sound very pleased for me,' he commented jeeringly, and Lizzy drew a shaky breath.

'Aileen won't make you happy,' she told him, knowing that it wouldn't make any difference, but needing to say it anyway.

'She'll make me happy the moment she says "I do".' Tye's voice was hard, his face closed. 'Barra will be mine, and no one will be able to take it away from me. That's all I need to make me happy.'

'If Barra is all you care about, then perhaps you're right.'

'Aileen and I will manage perfectly well without love,' he insisted. 'We're well matched. Neither of us is starting out with any expectations of true love and happy-ever-after, and we're likely to end up a lot happier than you when your romantic illusions are all you've got to keep you warm!'

Lizzy flinched at the savagery in his voice, and turned her face away. Hugging her arms together, she moved towards the steps, where the shadows were deeper and Tye wouldn't be able to see her expression.

'Wh-when will you get married?'

'There's no reason not to do it immediately. We could

fly up to Darwin at the end of this week, get married there and sort out all the legal stuff at the same time.'

'Aileen might prefer a proper wedding. They take some time to plan.'

'I'm not going through all that fuss,' said Tye curtly. 'It's a business arrangement, and I'm not going to pretend otherwise. Aileen won't mind as long as she gets a credit card to charge to my account.'

Maybe she wouldn't.

Lizzy took a deep breath as she turned to look at him once more. 'In that case, I may as well say goodbye now.'

'What do you mean, *goodbye*?'

'I'm going back to Perth first thing in the morning. I can get a lift with the caterers.'

'Tomorrow?' Tye sounded as if he had been knocked off balance. 'You can't go tomorrow!'

'Why not?'

'Because...because you're still working for me,' he snapped. 'I need you here.'

She smiled sadly. 'No, you don't. You've found a wife. I've done my job.'

'It's not finished yet.' A muscle was jerking furiously in Tye's jaw. 'There are still arrangements to be made.'

'You can make them with Aileen. It's nothing to do with me.'

'Oh, very well,' Tye snarled. 'Go, if you're so desperate to go, but you needn't think I'm paying you until after wedding!'

'Fine.' Somehow Lizzy managed to hang onto her precarious control as she turned to go. 'You've got my address in Perth. You can send a cheque there.'

Lizzy looked at the envelope a long time before she opened it. She knew what it was. Tye's bold black writing scrawled across the front, as if he had written her address in a fury.

Taking a deep breath, she slid her thumb under the flap and ripped it open before she had a chance to change her mind. Inside, just as she had dreaded, was a cheque.

So he was married.

Lizzy pressed her hand against her trembling mouth. Tye was married. Married. *Married.* She kept saying the word to herself, but her mind wouldn't accept it, even though she knew that it was true, even though she had been waiting for this moment ever since she had left Barra Creek the morning after the party.

Since then, Lizzy had been existing in a state of numb desperation. She had spent the journey back to Perth trying to convince herself that she would be fine as soon as she got home. She would pick up the pieces of her life and she would begin to forget Tye and Barra and the quiet creek.

Except it hadn't worked like that.

The harder Lizzy tried to forget, the more intensely she missed him, and the bleaker the aching, yawning emptiness inside her. She felt fragile, like a piece of porcelain webbed with tiny cracks, ready to shatter into a thousand pieces at the slightest blow.

Like getting Tye's cheque in the post. Like knowing that he was married after all.

Desolation gripped Lizzy by the throat, and she dropped the cheque, hugging her arms around her as if to stop herself falling apart. Why had she refused Tye when he asked her to marry him? So what if he didn't love her? At least she could have been with him. She could have had a lifetime to teach him how to love and to make him happy.

It could have been her, standing beside him, holding out her left hand and watching as Tye slid the ring onto her finger. It could have been her, waking up beside him at Barra and knowing that she would never have to leave.

But it hadn't been her. It had been Aileen.

Lizzy buried her head in her arms and wept.

When the phone rang that evening, she almost didn't answer it, but she had forgotten to switch on her answer-machine, and eventually she dragged herself over to pick it up. She had to get on with her life some time, and it might as well be now.

It was her mother, ringing with a familiar complaint that she was always the last person to know what her daughters were doing. 'I wouldn't even have known that you were back in Perth if I hadn't met Karen in Mathison,' she grumbled.

'Karen who?' said Lizzy without much interest.

'You know, *Karen*! Karen the cook,' her mother prompted. 'At Barra?'

Lizzy's throat closed at the mere mention of Barra. 'Oh…yes.'

'I must say, I think you might have told us you were leaving, Lizzy. Why do you never tell us what you're doing? I thought you were working for Tye Gibson!'

'I was,' Lizzy managed to say, 'but it was just a temporary thing. I…finished my contract…a couple of weeks ago.'

'I don't blame you,' said her mother candidly. 'According to Karen, he's been impossible ever since you left. She can't wait for him to go back to the States. Although whether she'll still have a job is—'

'What?' Lizzy interrupted as her mother's words sank in. 'What did you just say, Mum?'

'I said that Karen will be pleased when Tye Gibson goes back to the States,' her mother repeated obediently. 'Didn't you know?'

Lizzy felt cold. Tye couldn't go to America. Tye needed to be at Barra. What had gone wrong?

'But...I thought he was getting married,' she said blankly.

Really? Her mother was instantly alert at this new piece of gossip. 'Who to?'

'To Aileen Rogers.'

Her mother was genuinely astonished. 'Whatever gave you that idea? No, Aileen's taken up with Barry Pearse, and his family aren't at all pleased about it, I can tell you!'

'He's not married?' said Lizzy slowly.

'Barry? He's divorced...you know that!'

'Not Barry. Tye.' Her tongue felt thick and unwieldy in her mouth just saying his name.

'Well, if he is, he's kept it pretty quiet. Karen certainly doesn't know anything about it.'

'But he has to be married!' Lizzy leapt to her feet and began pacing the room, hardly aware of what she was saying. 'It's June the first today. He's only got a few days. He *can't* not be married!'

There was a puzzled silence at the other end of the line. 'Lizzy, what are you talking about?'

Lizzy took a deep breath, suddenly aware of just what she needed to do. 'Mum, I'm coming up first thing in the morning,' she said, ignoring her mother's question. 'Can I borrow your car?'

Lizzy parked the car in the shade and sat for a while looking at the homestead. She hadn't told Tye that she was coming. She hadn't even thought about what she

was going to say to him. All she knew was that she had
to see him.

If he was there.

What if he had already gone? A sudden chill trickled
down Lizzy's spine at the thought that she might be too
late, and she got quickly out of the car.

There was no one around as she climbed the steps to
the verandah and pulled open the screen door. It clattered
behind her in the silence. She walked down the long
corridor, her heels clicking on the polished wooden floor,
until she reached Tye's office.

The door was closed, but when Lizzy leant her ear
against it she could just make out the sound of his voice.
Her heart twisted at the familiar tones, and she straightened as the air evaporated from her lungs. He was there.

Moistening her lips, she took a shaky breath and
knocked on the door.

'Come in.'

Lizzy wiped her suddenly damp hand on her trousers
and laid it on the handle. She hesitated.

'Come in!'

The increasing irritation in his voice was oddly reassuring. It was Tye, all right. Lizzy opened the door and
walked in.

He was sitting in his swivelling director's chair with
his back to her, a cordless phone to his ear, and he was
in the middle of a conversation that her knock had evi-
dently interrupted. Curiously calm now that she was
there, Lizzy waited for him to notice her. It was enough
just to be in the same room as him, to know that a few
steps would take her to his side.

As if sensing her patience, Tye swung round to see
her standing in the middle of the room, in narrow white
trousers and a violet top, her blonde hair tumbling about

her face and her eyes very blue. Shock and something else flared in his face before the iron control closed over his expression, and he checked the sudden movement that would have taken him to his feet.

'I'll call you back,' he said into the phone, and switched it off without waiting for a reply. Carefully, he laid it on the desk, as if afraid that a sudden movement would make Lizzy disappear.

Lizzy's heart was slamming against her ribs, and she stared hungrily back at Tye as he got slowly to his feet. He looked older, she thought, devouring the sight of him with her eyes. Older and wearier, and there were new harsh lines around his mouth.

'Didn't you get my cheque?'

Lizzy was thrown by the brusqueness of the question that broke the simmering silence, and it took her a few moments to realise what he was talking about. 'Yes, I got it,' she said.

'It was what we agreed,' he said, almost defiantly.

'No, it wasn't.'

He stared at her, then his mouth twisted in a disillusioned smile. 'Don't tell me,' he said bitterly. 'You want more money?'

Lizzy shook her head. 'I don't want any,' she told him. 'We agreed that you would pay me when you were married, and you're not, are you?'

There was a pause. The grey eyes narrowed warily. 'No,' he admitted at last.

'Did Aileen refuse you after all?'

She thought at first that Tye wasn't going to answer. 'I didn't ask her,' he said in the end.

'Why not?'

This time he really didn't answer. Shoving his hands

in his pockets, he hunched his shoulders and turned away.

'What are you doing here, Lizzy?' he asked after a moment.

'I came to ask you something.'

'What is it?' He sounded flat, almost defeated.

'Will you marry me?'

There was a long, long pause. Tye stood utterly still before, very cautiously, he turned back to face her. *'What?'* he said softly.

Lizzy clutched her hands together. 'I asked you to marry me,' she said, amazed at how steady her voice sounded.

'Lizzy…' He took an involuntary step towards her, and then stopped himself. 'Why?'

She swallowed. 'Because you belong at Barra Creek. I…I can't bear to think of you having to leave here again.'

'You'd do that for me?' said Tye incredulously. 'You'd give up everything you believe in, everything you've always dreamt about, everything you've ever wanted?'

Lizzy avoided his eyes. 'Maybe I don't want what I always thought I wanted any more,' she said in a low voice. 'Maybe my dreams have changed.'

'You don't believe in true love any more?'

'Yes, I do. I just don't believe that it has to be perfect.'

Clutching her arms together, Lizzy walked over to the window. She stood, looking out, wondering just what to tell Tye, until it dawned on her that all she had to tell him was the truth.

'I don't think you're perfect,' she said, quite easily after all. 'You're not at all the kind of man I used to dream about falling in love with. You're infuriating and pig-headed and impossible to please. I don't agree with half the things you do or half the things you think. I don't even know why I'm in love with you. I just know I am.'

She turned back to face Tye. He was watching her with an indecipherable expression that almost made her lose her nerve, but she had told him so much, she might as well tell him the rest.

'I know you don't love me, Tye,' she went on, taking a steadying breath. 'I used to think that a one-sided marriage would be unbearable. I thought I wanted someone to adore me and think I was perfect too, but I don't want that any more. I just want you. These last two weeks in Perth, I've realised that living without you is much harder to bear. I kept telling myself that I could manage on my own, but I can't.'

Tye hadn't moved. 'Why didn't you tell me this before?' he asked.

'Because I thought it was too late,' said Lizzy. 'I thought you were going to marry Aileen. I'd had my chance, and I'd blown it. There hasn't been an hour since I left that I haven't regretted refusing to marry you,' she told him. 'When I heard that you hadn't married Aileen after all, I didn't want to miss another chance, and so...'

She lifted her hands a little helplessly and let them fall by her sides, unable to explain the driving sense of urgency that had possessed her. 'And so I came back,' she finished simply.

Still Tye said nothing. He was just standing there, looking at her, and Lizzy was suddenly swamped with the conviction that she had gone about things all wrong. She had messed up her last chance, she realised miserably. Far better to have played it cool and pretended that she wanted the money after all, instead of pouring out her feelings like that, rambling on about love and need and all the emotions that Tye loathed.

'I...I wouldn't expect anything from you,' she stumbled on, trying to make up for her mistake, although deep down she knew that it was too late. 'I'm not asking you to pretend, but if you marry me, I can give you what you really want.'

'Yes,' said Tye reflectively. 'I think you can.'

Relief rinsed the misery from Lizzy's face and her eyes glowed. 'Then you'll marry me next week?'

'No.'

'N-no?' Lizzy stared at him, not wanting to believe that she had heard him right, not wanting to understand the firm shaking of his head. 'But...but what about Barra?'

'I've already made my decision.'

A cold hand closed around Lizzy's heart. Why hadn't she thought of it before? Of *course* Tye wasn't going to give up Barra just like that. She swallowed hard. 'You've asked someone else?'

'No.'

'Then *why*?' she cried. 'There's still time. We could get married in a few days, and Barra would be yours. You could have all you've ever wanted!'

'Except that Barra *isn't* all I want,' said Tye.

He leant against his desk and folded his arms, his eyes never leaving Lizzy's face. 'I contacted Paul Gibson last week,' he went on conversationally. 'I told him that I wasn't going to fulfil my father's conditions and that Barra would belong to him next week. We had a long chat. He's in advertising and has absolutely no interest in owning a cattle station. He was appalled to learn that he might have to take responsibility for Barra, and he wanted to simply give Barra back to me, but in the end

I persuaded him to let me buy the station from him at the market price. He's entitled to the money under the terms of my father's will, and it's not as if I can't afford it. And this time Barra won't have any conditions attached to it.'

'So you don't need to get married after all?'

Tye looked at her. 'No.'

'I see.' Lizzy turned around so that he wouldn't see the desolation on her face. She took a deep breath and forced a cheery note into her voice. 'Well…I seem to have made a bit of a fool of myself, don't I?'

She didn't see Tye straighten, or the tenderness in his face as he walked over to her, but she felt his hands on her shoulders and she tensed. She couldn't bear his pity.

Ignoring her resistance, Tye slid his hands down her arms and took hold of her waist so that he could turn her to face him. 'I don't *need* to get married any more,' he said softly. 'That doesn't mean that I don't *want* to. I do.'

Rigidly aware of his touch, Lizzy stared up at him, bewilderment and hurt in her blue eyes. 'But you said—'

'I said I didn't want to marry you next week.' Tye let go of her waist to possess her hands in a strong clasp, and his eyes were warmer than Lizzy had ever seen them. 'I don't want Barra to be the reason we get married, Lizzy. I want you to marry me because I love you and need you, just as much as you love me…more, even.'

'You…love…me?' Lizzy repeated the words as if they didn't make any sense, and Tye smiled, a smile that cracked the film of icy despair that had encased her ever since she had said goodbye to him.

'Hopelessly,' he confirmed.

Warmth and wonder were trickling into Lizzy's sore heart, but she didn't dare let herself believe it, not yet. 'I thought you didn't believe in love?' she said, the wariness in her voice belied by the way her fingers were curling like bindweed around his.

'So did I,' said Tye. 'I'd never been in love before. I didn't know what was happening to me. I'd gotten so used to being independent, to believing that I didn't need anyone else, and then suddenly there you were, part of my life, so warm and funny and vibrant.'

His voice deepened as he lifted his hands to cradle her face very gently between his palms. 'So beautiful,' he added, tracing her cheekbones tenderly with his thumbs.

This couldn't be happening, thought Lizzy in daze. Enchantment was coiling around her like a web of gold, holding her captive while she drowned wonderingly in the loving warmth of his eyes. Released, her hands had clutched at his shirt, instinctively seeking the reassurance of his hard, strong body, anchoring herself to this new, wonderful reality, letting herself believe after all that this was real.

'I told myself that what I felt for you was just physical attraction,' Tye went on, gazing lovingly down into the dazzled blue eyes. 'I didn't expect it to last, but when I asked you to marry me and you refused, I was furious.

'It wasn't even as if you were in love with another man,' he pretended to grumble. 'I'd been rejected in favour of a dream! Of course, I told myself that I didn't care, and that Barra was all that mattered, but when you introduced me to all those women who could have helped me to get Barra, I couldn't concentrate.'

His lips grazed Lizzy's temple, drifted deliciously

down her cheek. 'How could I look at them,' he murmured, 'when you were beside me?'

He gathered her closer as he kissed his way to the sensitive skin just below her earlobe. 'When I could smell your perfume?' he whispered in her ear, lingering there as a shiver of pure pleasure snaked down Lizzy's spine.

'When every time I saw you I thought about how it felt to kiss you?' His kisses were enticing, tantalisingly soft, straying along her jaw until they found the corner of her mouth, where it curved upwards in an irresistible smile.

Joy was spilling along Lizzy's veins in a golden cascade, and she let out a sigh of bliss as she wound her arms around Tye's neck and turned her face so that their lips met at last and they could kiss—a long, hungry kiss that went on and on, broken by breathless, mumbled endearments, until Lizzy thought that she would faint with happiness.

'I never guessed,' she said when she could speak. She was sitting on Tye's lap by then, pressing desperate kisses against his throat, still hardly daring to believe that this was not a dream. 'I thought kissing me was just part of your strategy to find a bride.'

'It was in Sydney,' Tye confessed. He smoothed the hair tenderly from Lizzy's face and kissed her once more. 'But somehow everything seemed different when we were at Barra. It was so easy being with you. You weren't like anyone else I had ever met. You talked and you laughed and you made me see things I'd never seen before, and I was happy.

'I'd never been that happy before,' he told Lizzy, his grey eyes suddenly serious. 'I tried to persuade myself that it was because I was back at Barra, but it wasn't. It was because you were there. Do you remember that day at the waterhole?'

'Um...' Lizzy rolled up her eyes, pretending to think, but Tye wasn't fooled. He pulled her closer, kissing her eyes, her nose, her lips, while his hands teased her and made her squirm with desire.

'I know you remember,' he murmured into her throat, and Lizzy gave in.

'Every second,' she whispered back.

'I didn't really mean that to happen, but I couldn't keep my hands off you any longer, and when I kissed you it was as if everything fell into place. I couldn't believe it when you said no.'

Lizzy snuggled closer. 'I wish I hadn't.'

'It was a good lesson for me,' said Tye ruefully. 'I began to wonder if that kiss had meant the same to you, and of course I was too proud to ask. I'd never doubted myself before, but it seemed as if you were only interested in a job after all. And when we went to that rodeo...'

He trailed off, shaking his head at the memory. 'That was a bad day. I could see how much everyone cared about you, and how deeply they mistrusted me. For the first time, it bothered me that I was an outcast. Why would someone like you throw in your lot with me? I knew that money wouldn't win you.'

Tipping up Lizzy's chin, he made her look at him. 'You're the only reason I rode that bloody horse,' he told her with mock sternness. 'I wanted to prove to you that I could belong, and you weren't even watching!'

'I did watch!' Lizzy sat up in protest. 'I hated every moment of it! I was terrified that you were going to be hurt.'

'Well, you weren't there when I got off,' said Tye.

'You were with Gray Henderson, and as soon as I saw him I knew that he was everything I'd never be. *He* belonged. He was safe, he was kind, he was nice. He was everything a girl like you deserved.'

'Gray's all those things,' Lizzy agreed, settling back against Tye with a contented sigh. 'But he's not you.' She kissed him. 'Were you really jealous?'

Tye grinned at the pleased note in her voice and his arms tightened around her. 'I was beside myself,' he admitted, 'especially when I saw you with him again at the races. I was determined to find someone there, to prove to you and to myself that I didn't need you after all, but I barely spoke to Aileen before I made an excuse and rushed off to find where you'd gone.'

'But why were you so angry?'

'What did you expect? I'd been running around looking for you, and there you were, hugging Gray Henderson again. I felt as if I'd been punched in the stomach. And you...' Tye stroked her cheek '...you looked so unhappy. I was afraid that you might feel more for Gray than you wanted to admit. I just wanted to take you home and keep you to myself, but I'd committed myself to that wretched party, and there was still the problem of my father's will... I wasn't thinking straight, I'm afraid, and I took it out on you. I know I wasn't easy to live with that week.'

'Were you really going to ask Aileen to marry you?' asked Lizzy, remembering that bitter argument on the dark verandah.

'I only said that when you seemed so determined to go back to Perth and set up your own business,' said Tye. 'Then there didn't seem much point in *not* asking her, and I guess I didn't want you to think that I cared about you one way or the other. And by then I'd convinced myself that Barra was all that mattered.'

'But you never asked her?'

'No. I went to see her, but when it came to it, I couldn't do it. God knows what Aileen thought I was doing there, but I knew at that moment that I couldn't bear to marry anyone but you. I'd thought that Barra would be enough, but it wasn't. I didn't want it if I couldn't have you.'

Tye picked up Lizzy's hand and turned it over, pressing a kiss into her palm. 'It was only when you'd gone that I knew how much I loved you, Lizzy,' he told her quietly. 'I missed you. Barra was empty without you. I kept looking for you, waiting to see you coming through the screen door, or putting on your hat. Everything reminded me of you. I'd sit on the verandah and think of you curled up in a chair. I'd go down to the creek and remember you walking through the trees. A fence would remind me of the way you'd struggled with all that barbed wire and never complained once about getting your hands dirty. And when I looked at the sky, all I could see were your eyes.

'It was a week before I gave in,' he went on after a moment. 'I realised that Barra wasn't going to mean anything unless you were there to share it with me. That's when I rang Paul Gibson.'

'Why didn't you come and tell me then?' asked Lizzy.

'Because I knew that you wouldn't believe me if I told you that I loved you before I was forty. Even if by some miracle you'd said yes, you'd always wonder at the back of your mind if I'd only married you because of Barra.'

Tye held her face between his hands. 'That's not why

I'm marrying you, Lizzy, you have to believe that,' he said with sudden urgency. 'I love you.'

'And I love you,' she said, and kissed him.

It was some time before she could speak again, and she rested her face blissfully against Tye's throat. 'It does seem a bit extravagant, to buy back Barra when we're getting married anyway,' she commented with a long sigh of sheer happiness. 'Why don't we do it next week, before your birthday?'

'That's not enough time to arrange everything,' he pointed out, and she sat back in surprise.

'All we need is a licence. That won't take long.'

'What about your dress? And the flowers? We need to book the church in Mathison and make sure everyone can come. It all takes time.'

'But you hate weddings!'

Tye pulled her back against him. 'I won't hate this one,' he said. 'I want it to be perfect.'

'If you're not careful, you're going to turn into a romantic,' Lizzy teased him, putting her arms back round his neck.

'Don't you want a proper wedding?'

'Of course I do,' she said, kissing him again, 'but there is just *one* problem.'

'There is?'

'You haven't actually asked me to marry you yet.'

Tye's arms closed around her. 'I seem to remember that I've already asked you twice,' he pointed out as he kissed her back. 'And both times you said no.'

'Well, this time I'll say yes,' Lizzy promised.

'In that case, my darling, for the *third* time...'

What happens when you suddenly
discover your happy twosome is about
to turn into a...*family?*
Do you laugh?
Do you cry?
Or...do you get married?

The answer is all of the above—and plenty more!

Share the laughter and tears with
Harlequin Romance® as these
unsuspecting couples have to be

When parenthood takes you by surprise!

Authors to look out for include:

**Caroline Anderson—DELIVERED: ONE FAMILY
Barbara McMahon—TEMPORARY FATHER
Grace Green—TWINS INCLUDED!
Liz Fielding—THE BACHELOR'S BABY**

Available wherever Harlequin books are sold.

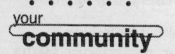

*Harlequin truly does
make any time special....
This year we are celebrating
weddings in style!*

There's more...

To help us celebrate, we want you to tell us how wearing the Harlequin wedding gown will make your wedding day special. As the grand prize, Harlequin will offer one lucky bride the chance to **"Walk Down the Aisle" in the Harlequin wedding gown!**

There's more...

For her honeymoon, she and her groom will spend five nights at the **Hyatt Regency Maui.** As part of this five-night honeymoon at the hotel renowned for its romantic attractions, the couple will enjoy a candlelit dinner for two in Swan Court, a sunset sail on the hotel's catamaran, and duet spa treatments.

To enter, please write, in, 250 words or less, how wearing the Harlequin wedding gown will make your wedding day special. The entry will be judged based on its emotionally compelling nature, its originality and creativity, and its sincerity. This contest is open to Canadian and U.S. residents only and to those who are 18 years of age and older. There is no purchase necessary to enter. Void where prohibited. See further contest rules attached. Please send your entry to:

Walk Down the Aisle Contest

In Canada	In U.S.A.
P.O. Box 637	P.O. Box 9076
Fort Erie, Ontario	3010 Walden Ave.
L2A 5X3	Buffalo, NY 14269-9076

You can also enter by visiting www.eHarlequin.com
Win the Harlequin wedding gown and the vacation of a lifetime!
The deadline for entries is October 1, 2001.

PHWDACONT1

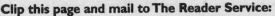

LONG, TALL TEXANS

EMMETT, REGAN & BURKE

New York Times
extended list bestselling author

Diana PALMER

**returns to Jacobsville, Texas, in this special
collection featuring rugged heroes, spirited
heroines and passionate love stories told
in her own inimitable way!**

Coming in May 2001 only from Silhouette Books!

®
Silhouette
™
Where love comes alive™